IN A
FLASH
2024

Other titles by
Danielle Ackley-McPhail

The Eternal Cycle Series
Yesterday's Dreams
Tomorrow's Memories
Today's Promise

The Eternal Wanderings Series
Eternal Wanderings

The Bad-Ass Faerie Tale Series
The Halfling's Court
The Redcap's Queen
The High King's Fool
(forthcoming)

Baba Ali and the Clockwork Djinn
(with Day Al-Mohamed)

The Literary Handyman
More Tips from the Handyman
Build-A-Book Workshop

The Ginger KICK! Cookbook
Auntie D's Recipes

Short Fiction
A Legacy of Stars
Transcendence
Consigned to the Sea
The Fox's Fire
The Kindly One
Dawns a New Day
Echoes of the Divine
The Die Is Cast
(with Mike McPhail)

eSPEC BOOKS

IN A FLASH

2024

Danielle Ackley-McPhail

eSpec Books
Pennsville, NJ

PUBLISHED BY
eSpec Books LLC
Danielle McPhail,
Publisher
PO Box 242,
Pennsville, New Jersey 08070
www.especbooks.com

ISBN: 978-1-956463-07-1
ISBN (ebook): 978-1-956463-06-4

Copy Editor: Greg Schauer
Cover Art and Design: Mike McPhail, McP Digital Graphics
Interior Design: Danielle McPhail

To Bill Hicks, for all our time as NOVLs.

CONTENTS

Part III - Realism

Part IV - Science Fiction

FANTASY

TO BRANDISH A WHITE LADLE

A Chronicle of the Four Lunch Ladies of the Apocalypse

YOU WOULD HAVE THOUGHT IT WAS THE END OF DAYS.
Really.
It was that bad.

Not the situation, that weren't nothing much. But the ruckus... That little missy needed to check her vapors at the door. Dina Lynn Washnowski sat in the middle of controlled chaos bawling her eyes out over some limp little fish fingers. Apparently, in elementary school, missing out on pizza day was a cataclysm. What can I say? It's her own fault for fooling around with her friends instead of getting into line.

First-grade problems, I tell you.

Just the next table over from her, I watched Sally Parker share out her little square of pizza between her two sisters, Mary and Abigail, because their momma couldn't afford more than one lunch ticket. I could tell from here she'd taken the smallest slice to boot. Then she divided everything else on the tray the same way.

Bet you they would have loved to have those fish fingers...

Dina Lynn just kept bawling. Nobody paid her any mind except for me.

I shook my head and kept doing what I was doing. A couple of the little monsters brought up their milk or apples or what have you—the healthy stuff they couldn't be bothered to eat— and left it for whoever else wanted it. I waited for them to mosey on back to their seats before scooping up their leavings and wandering over to the Parker sisters. Without a word, or even looking at those sweet girls, I set the bounty on the table and walked away.

What's that? Who am I?

Why, my friends call me 'Bert. Short for Alberta. But the kids call me Lady Bert. Short for Lunch Lady. Nice to meetcha.

Me, by the way, I used to be just like Sally Parker. Some ways, I like to think I still am. That little lady has a quiet, dignified manner about her... okay, so maybe I'm not so much like her in that regard, but when it comes to charity and compassion...

Guess I should've known better than to turn my back on the room.

Seems on one side of the cafeteria, the future cheerleaders of America smuggled in an Ouija board or something. While on the other, the future Geek Squad crowd broke out their illicit video games the moment they inhaled their lunches. Maybe it was a coincidence, but the air began to buzz and crackle across my skin, I swear, like two cosmic forces crossed streams or something.

Miss Sylvie stood at the entrance to the serving line. A faint frown creased her brow as she scanned the room. I worked my way past the tables and back toward the kitchen to stand beside her. We were quite the pair, her petite and pale and willow-switch thin, her braided hair as black and shiny as a licorice twist; and me, as plump and rosy as a Georgia peach, with my corn-silk golden hair in a stylish up-do. We shared the frown, though.

Whatever charged the air, the kids felt it. You could tell by the way they fussed at one another.

"What's goin' on?"

I swear I'm a smack that girl silly someday. Tabby came up sudden-like behind us, tugging at her spiky lime-sherbet hair, and snapping the gum she wasn't supposed to be chewing. She wasn't much older than the kids sitting out at the tables, but she was one of us. A Lunch Lady-in-Waiting, as I liked to think of her. She had a lot to learn but certainly seemed willing. I liked the way she looked out for the kids, not quite leaning on the bullies, but always making sure they knew she was watching. Couldn't hardly tell if she was helping the kids or hanging out with them, but she got her work done, and the kids got fed, that's what counted.

"Well?"

"Don't know," I murmured, rubbing down the hairs prickling on my arms. "Best go get the Sarge."

That would be Josephine... but don't you ever dare call her that. At best, she won't answer. At worse, she will.

With another snap of her gum, Tammy went to comply. Better her than me, Sarge had a temper when you interrupted her paperwork. Just like the army, a well-run cafeteria ran on paperwork. Or was that ran away from paperwork? Honestly, I can't keep it straight. I'm just here to make sure the food gets eaten and not tossed around.

The master sergeant came striding out of the kitchen looking tall, lean, and tough as whipcord. And more than a little pissed. Well... she weren't a master sergeant anymore, but when you wear a rank as long as she did, it soaks into your bones and there it stays like set-in gravy that ain't nothing gonna get out. If the lunchroom had a bouncer, she was it. Right now, she wore her hard-core sergeant face, looking mighty tired and out of patience with the horse pucky going on. Her silver-shot crimson curls sat close to her head, like a helmet, and in her right hand she held a white plastic ladle like a baton... or a club, to be more honest.

That's our Josephine... always ready to do battle...

You just hush up, and don't you go telling her I called her that!

Now, like I was saying, *Sarge* stood there, poise and ready like she was inspecting the troops.

Of course, don't you know, that's when all hell's bells broke loose...

Three sets of double doors led into the multi-purpose room— that's what you call it when the lunchroom's got to be nearly everything else as well. Every blessed one of those doors flew open at once with a bang you just would not believe.

You thought there was yelling before? Let me just tell you... you don't know yelling until a flood of goblins comes tumbling into the room in the middle of April like it was the end of October instead. Kids know darned well when Halloween is and when it isn't.

That's when our Josephine starts whipping her ladle around and busting out the big guns with her drill instructor voice,

"Lunch monitors, get your children into the teachers' lounge, now! Ladies..." That's us... "You're with me!"

Now, don't go thinking that left us all on our own. There's not a teacher worth their salt that wouldn't stand between their kids and danger... especially when faced with the prospect of being crammed in a tiny room with what had to be at least a hundred children during what was supposed to be their break.

Yeah, I'd face the goblins too. Just saying...

Of course, none of us are foolish enough to face an army of goblins with just a single ladle and our bare hands. Aren't too many knives in a school kitchen... the board of ed kind of plans it so they aren't needed—don't ask me why—but there are plenty of really hard plastic trays. I took care of arming the troops, while Tabby hurried over to the PE closet (what part of multi-purpose room did you not understand?) By the time I ran out of what I now like to call whack-paddles to put into the teachers hands, Tabby and Miss Sylvie had busted out the dodge balls and I know for a fact those hard little suckers were just filled up with air.

It. Was. Glorious.

Between Sarge whaling through the horde swinging her ladle and the teachers flailing about with their whack-paddles and the rest of us beaming those stupid suckers for all we were worth with properly hard dodge balls. Why, we didn't even have to threaten to unleash those kids on their sorry, invading buttocks...

Haven't a clue where those goblins came from, haven't a clue where they went, but when we peeked outside those busted-out doors... well, let's just say it's a good thing we had plenty of room to hunker down. We closed those doors nice and tight and chained them like we was closing up for the night before herding our own little monsters back to their tables and trying to pretend like not a thing was strange.

You'll excuse me though, for heading into that kitchen just as soon as I was able to find something a touch more intimidating than a ball or a whack-paddle to keep to hand.

After all, we can't all be Sergeant Jo.

❈❈

Don't you know... that Dina Lynn sat right back down where she started, bawling even harder because some stupid-ass goblin from beyond ate her mangled fish fingers. I guess second choice beats nothing at all...

With long, ground-eating strides, Sergeant Jo went back to the kitchen, coming back out not ten minutes later with a Styrofoam plate in her hand. Crossing the multi-purpose room, she plopped that plate in front of the blotchy faced little darling. Dina Lynn looked up at her with big glistening eyes, then down at the plate holding two English muffins from breakfast smeared with sauce and topped with melty cheese.

"Buck up, little girl. It's not the end of the world."

Letting out one more sniffly little hiccup, the child smiled, all sunshine and puppies, and started chomping on those makeshift pizzas like all was now right with her world.

In my head I could hear Sergeant Jo's unspoken words...

Not yet.

BROOKLYN BORNE

In Sheepshead Bay
a rift in time
did open up
the wyrdinq way
laying bare
the thoughts of man
breaking loose
their mortal clay
adrift in myst
of eldritch light
the way is lost
'tween night and day
unless ye pledge
to elfling lords
ye'll meet the wrath
of Brooklyn's fae

THE HEART OF THE SUN

THE AIR CRACKLED THE DAY BORVO SAW HER IN THE PUBLIC SQUARE. From his haven in the sky, the sun god looked down as the flicker of her unexpected flame caught his eye. He watched in fascination as she spun and gestured and clutched at anyone who drew near to where she stood in the Place of Declaration. They all ignored her. Or brusquely snatched themselves away. Not one looked at the passion burning like the seams of a lava flow beneath her skin. He had to wonder what raged inside her to ignite such a powerful beacon. Whatever it was, it astounded him that those she caught did not burn with it the moment she touched them. She did not speak, beyond the eloquence of her eyes, but never stopped clutching. Not as long as he watched, nor would she, he suspected, far after.

He was wrong.

The pompous fools passing around her on their way to whatever triviality ruled their day eluded her grasping hands deftly. She persisted, but they circled wide around. Borvo knew she would not chase them. Too much pride sizzled in her to bear such shame. Instead, she drew herself up and looked to the sky.

Borvo went still and his own gaze flared as she seemed to look right at him. The little one raised an unvoiced cry in entreaty, borne on the currents of that liquid fire coursing beneath her skin, head flung back, her arms lifted wide, as if she would take to his skies. But no... The earth bound her too heavily in flesh. Her shoulders slumped as her eyes drifted closed, banking that intriguing fire. Silent tears fell across her cheeks like hot ash.

The sight of her submission enraged Borvo until the heat of his displeasure beat down upon those below. They wilted at his wrath, struggling to go about their business, their flesh turning pink and angry as sweat dotted their brow. But not his little one. She straightened beneath his touch, smiled at the radiance of his rays. When her eyes opened once more, their passion rekindled.

Her lips began to move fast, like the flicker of a wind-whipped fire, but Borvo could not hear her words. Reaching out, he sent tendrils of sunbeams to wrap about her limbs, charged with catching the faintest whisper.

There was none.

Puzzled, Borvo looked into the shallow souls of the people for some answer and read their offense. They ignored her, for she had no voice, no words, nothing but silence and passion and the energy of her movements to convince them. In their eyes, she was less than them, and thus beneath their notice. Flawed. *Different.* Something they should not acknowledge or draw near, lest her infirmity corrupt their own worth.

And then Borvo knew. He knew what ignited her soul and sparked her gaze. The little one declared herself, shouted to the world without words: See me! I am here! And the sun god's heart answered, his warmth folding her in its embrace.

"Little one," Borvo whispered into her soul, "surely you are born of fire, not mere earth. Come to me." And then he reached into her core and liberated her flame.

The mortals gasped and flung themselves back as a pyre ignited where Kenna stood in the Place of Declaration. And from its flame came the sound of glorious singing as her silenced voice was set free. Wings of fire unfurled and Borvo's love took to the sky.

SWEET LIAM ROANES

You left behind a trail
... footprints in the sand
... ripples through the waves
... blissful agony etched upon my heart
Leading me to the precipice.

Your calls were a siren song
... drifting on the wind,
... rising from the surf
... echoing in my cries,
Tempting me at the cliff's edge

Lost in the memory of your skin
... like cream silk against my lips
... like slick grey velvet beneath my fingertips
... like salty sweetness tipping my tongue
Drawing me into your madness.

Why I did not notice
The melancholy edge to your laughter
... the sorrow underlying the joy
in your endless eyes?

Blessed of the divine children
Cursed immortal soul
Call down a storm upon this shore
That nature may cry my tears
For I have lost my heart to a selkie,
And I've lost my selkie to the sea.

Previously published in *No Longer Dreams*, Lite Circle Books.

ENCHAINEDMENT

EVERY YEAR THE METAL LINKS ENCROACHED ON HER DOMAIN, drawing tighter and tighter until they cut into her flesh. The spell was ancient, from the time when the Hindereds walked brazenly across the landscape, dominating the Green, dictating where and how they would flourish. The Hindereds who could not—would not—heed the pleas of the Green for peace between them.

Her limbs shuddered and a whisper of leaves wept with her. Intrusive metal made her blood burn as another year passed. It was like an anchor, forever locking her in place. With each passing day she lost more contact with her skin; it was a vague tingling to her now as she found herself locked deeper and deeper within, bound by the chain-linked fence around her heart.

Daire towered above the landscape, taller than the crumbling structures of the Hindereds; her girth wider than fifteen of them could reach around with their stunted limbs. Around her the world was desolate, but once again it belonged to the Green— what remained of them. The Hindereds had faded away, removed from the Cycle by their own hand. Beneath her feet still rested a few scattered bones, crumbling, feeding the earth with their precious calcium.

And here she was, alive to see the day when the Green were free to reclaim the glorious earth... and here she was... locked within her tree by binding metal at the core, unable to venture out and dance in the dust of their oppressors.

TO REACH
FOR DISTANT SHORES
A Tale from the World of the Silver Moon

THE ANSWERS TO MY DREAMS WERE BROUGHT TO ME BY A FLASH storm come up from the south off the sea—violent, sudden, unexpected. The winds rarely drove from that direction, but when they did, it was gloriously primal. I could feel them in the delicate bones of my body, like the warning my whisker hairs sent when something dangerous loomed close by.

While my sisters and brothers dove down deep at the threat of the storm, I wended my way upward, to peer from the lee of the rocks jutting from the slapping waters, my eyes trained on the water's surface and the skies, avidly watching for the signs that would come swift and sudden and much too late for any about on the surface to heed. In the distance, barely heard, the air rumbled warning of the tempest's approach. With vague interest, I noticed narrow, oblong bladders high up in the sky, floating like the jellies beneath the waves, right down to the tendrils dangling from their core. Tiny trailers of electric static crackled like an eel's warning across the bladder's skin before the energy was gone, dispersed on the quickening wind.

Again my bones shivered as the storm drew ever closer. This was the moment when down close to the water, the air felt too still. My eyes scanned the sea, drawn by vibrations on the surface. To my left, a large mass drifted by like a rare leviathan risen from the depths in the dark hour to let the light of the unseen moon brush its skin. It was a made thing, a ship, filled with man-things scurrying about at this first hint of the coming storm. As the vessel passed, thunder rumbled faintly in the distance, popping closer and closer. The rapidly darkening clouds lit up, and sudden trails of lightning danced down from the sky, colliding with each other and the mass on the water, high up where thin, straight branches rose like webbed fingers to touch the air.

I watched with eager eyes, my breath barely rippling the froth on the waves. My hands gripped tight to the moss-coated rocks as my fins were nibbled clean by the tiny fish living in the shoals, poised to escape beneath the depths when the heavens finally crashed down to whip the waves into a frenzy. I left my leaving long, clinging in place as the air charged and crackled, and thunderclouds of a sudden boiled up on the horizon. With a gleeful laugh, I dove deep and fast before the storm front blanketed the world above.

None on water or in air saw mercy from that tempest. I came up to the shallows when the worst passed, eager to see the evidence of the storm's might. With care, I darted from mass to mass, just beneath the water. All I found was broken by the punch of the waves and wind, bitten by the power of the lightning. Fragments of those odd conveyances rained down, caught and cradled a moment before being swallowed by the sea.

I turned my attention to the masters of those vessels. The bodies I left for the currents to slurp down or batter upon the distant sands as they may. There was one I came across with warmth yet in his veins. I wrapped both arms around and drew him down with me. Beneath the runnels of blood and scraggled hair, there was something on his face that spoke of fear. He jerked and thrashed as the waves closed overhead, his odd, split tail flailing uselessly against my single powerful one. I murmured reassurances in his ear, but he continued to struggle. Grimacing, I tightened my grip and swam more swiftly to gain us the sanctuary of my private grotto.

I held an eager breath. Never had I had this chance before. To speak to one who made their home above the water. One who knew of the sky jellies. There was little doubt of communication between us. In my long life, I had traveled far and listened well. I was confident I could speak and understand every language the man-things spoke near the sea—which was to say all of them.

I knew what I would ask him. The only thing I cared to ask him: *How? How do you reach the sky?* It was my dearest dream to take my place up there, to gain those distant shores and swim the waters of the unseen moon. I dreamt of dancing with the lightning, of climbing its jagged bolts into the heavens. There were oceans there. I could not see them, but I could feel their call in the shivers down my scales and the tremors through my whisker hairs. I had no doubt those waters were there. After all, look how much spray rained down to mingle here below.

The lightning climbed up into the sky. Those like the one wrapped in my arms rode the winds. Perhaps the air-jellies were the key to gaining the clouds. This one held the secret. He *would* give it up. My egg sibs scoffed, but I would not rest until I was as cradled by those waters above as I was by my own sea.

And here was my chance to discover the secret to making this so.

But my effort was for naught. By the time we shook off the water's clinging, and I drew the stranger from above up upon my own hidden sands deep below, the warmth had fled him. I stared at his peculiar face and my teeth gnashed, jagged edge against jagged edge. I traced the plump curve of his now-blue lips and peered into strange, near-flat eyes, gone blood-shot and lifeless as if my answers were written there. They were not. But something did glitter slightly lower. I reached out, pushing aside the odd flaps that covered his chest like a skin torn loose and let flop to either side. Beneath was a wonder. It was an object like lightning-struck sand only smooth and straight and clear. Something encapsulated within glowed faintly. I lifted the thing away, breaking the thin strap it hung from around the dead one's neck. And none too soon.

A splash behind me betrayed an intrusion. "Your bottom-feeder tendencies are showing, my dear."

Phin. Like a case of scale rot, that one had plagued me ever since we were fingerlings. Even in the sac, he was rotten, I was sure. Someday, when I spawn my young, I would eat any eggs that held darkness such as his, for Phin had one goal: by word and deed, inflict what harm he may and often. His disdainful tone sent my lips into a snarl. As if I would feed upon a thinking being.

Before he spied it, I slipped my prize into the kelp bands I'd strung about my waist for carrying such things as I did not wish to hold in my hands. I then turned and glared at where he lounged, flukes in the water, arms on the sands, bracing him up. As ever, his eyes were mocking.

He could not have noticed my expression.

Not when he was too busy staring up and down the length of me, eyes lingering in the region of my pelvic fins. Hissing with annoyance and distaste, I heaved the strange one to my shoulder. With a wiggle of my fins and tail, I shoved past my egg brother—we were sheltered in the same nest, though not spawned from the same source—before sliding into the water, hauling the corpse to the grotto entrance where I let the eager current reclaim its prize.

Unburdened but still weighed down, I undulated upward. The surface was choppy yet, dotted with flotsam not claimed by the depths, but the clouds had vanished as quickly as they'd come, leaving the sky deep and dark and finely speckled like a dolphin. I let my head fall back, eyes closed, and breathed deep of the cleansed, ozone-scented air, savoring the lingering taste of saltwater tinged with fresh-churned kelp on my lips. Slowly my muscles unbunched. My eyes opened to scan the sky. To the left, high up, there was a patch seemingly void of stars. A dark cloud? One of the sky jellies? I could not say, but without a doubt, I could dream. With a few powerful strokes of my tail, I swam again toward the rocks, hauled myself up, and let the moon-beams caress my skin. I looked up to the larger moon, the one all could see. Its touch was cool, soft. Pleasant, but nothing more. The other... the hidden moon... my skin and scales glowed with the charge it imbued. Warmth bathed me on the inside, despite the chill of the night.

Someday... Someday I would gain that vaunted moon's shores and swim in its vibrant seas.

Forcing my gaze down and away lest I remain mesmerized for longer than was safe, I looked down to the object tucked within my kelp bands. My hand trembled as I drew it out with care. It was fine, more delicate than I would have thought possi-ble. I could imagine neither its purpose nor manner of creation. I had taken it because it caught my eye. I kept it for it seemed a treasure, something of value to the lost soul I had claimed it from. Perhaps it would serve a purpose for me, as lure or boon to one from his world who might aid me. I secured it once more, not wanting the jealous waves to claim my prize.

That was when I heard it. A broken sound. A weak one. It was foreign even to me, who had ventured forth through all the earthly seas available to me—which was to say, all of them. I was a powerful swimmer.

My dorsal fronds stiffened, not quite billowing as they would beneath the waves, but nonetheless, they snapped at the air in eager anticipation. This was a new thing. I angled my head to capture the sound. To pinpoint the source. It had something of a seal's bark—were the seal half dead. And something of the seagull's caw, only much less demanding. I could not for a moment imagine what made such a sound. Taut with the need to know, I drew myself across the rocks, up through the crevice that split this oceanic outcrop. I was silent as I moved, the muscles in my tail bunching to push against the rock, aiding my arms as they may. As I drew closer to the sound, I slowed my motions. A tall, thin spire of rock jutted high overhead. With care, I placed my webbed fingers against its jagged mass and pulled myself up to peer around the bulk of it.

The water glittered in the moonlight as it could not hope to beneath the sun, else I would not have noticed. Breaking up that liquid shimmer was an odd form clinging to the base of the outcrop, half in and half out of the waves. It humped first large, then smaller, holding to the rocks as tight as a barnacle did. There was the odd glimmer as the moon stroked something wet and sleek, but only in patches as if the form were not all of one thing.

I almost lost my grip and tumbled down as suddenly a different, higher wail rose, piercing my delicate ears clear through. And then I saw the one form was two, small huddled against the large. My pelvic fins fluttered instinctually. I watched as the bigger of the two pulled the other close to shelter against her... for her it was, I could see as the moon now caressed the paleness of her face. The little one looked up, and a sound escaped me. It was a boy-thing, little lips full and flat eyes familiar, though lacking the tinge of blood-red last seen upon the eyes of another face. Were the sea kinder, I could see this one might grow into the man-thing I'd gripped in my arms not long ago.

Perhaps it was my earlier thoughts of spawning, but an ache settled in my chest to see that young one at the mercy of the sea. I leaned closer, my head tilted for a better view, my ear hole bent toward them to pick up the words drifting on the night's breeze.

"He said that he would find us... he promised. If anything happened to the ship," the woman-thing murmured through cracked lips. Her words drifted, broken and as faint as the sounds she'd first made. "Find a place of safety, he said and signal him. He will come. He promised. But the flare... it's gone." Her one hand came up briefly to touch an object around her neck. From a familiar strap hung the fragments of what seemed to be a cousin to the object hidden in my kelp bands. As the woman-thing slid deeper in the water, she scrambled to cling to the rocks once more.

More of the tortured sounds, point and counterpoint, high voice and low. Though the sounds hurt my ears, I remain perched in my crevice, oddly captivated by the scene below. As I stayed there, the night air brushed over my form, gentle but persistent, until my skin and scales itched and twitched and tightened enough to bring me to wailing myself. The depths called to me, soothing and wet, cool and dark, and yet I remained until I spied the boy-thing slide into the grip of the waves. The woman-thing cried out and dove fearlessly after, in several long moments surfacing with her sputtering young. He choked and gasped as I have never heard a creature come from the sea. Great wracking coughs spewed water upon the rocks. My gaze went to his neck. I gasped myself, and my gills twitched in empathy when realization dawned: as the fish remained ever below, these man-things thrived only above. My mouth gaped with remorse as my eyes were opened to what I had done in drawing the man-thing down beneath the waves. I had borne no malice, yet like Phin, I'd wreaked great harm. Even could I wrest the man-thing from the sea, the deed could not be undone. He would not breathe again, nor return to these steadfastly waiting. But there was one thing I could do in restitution. My numb fingers slid down to grip the rod still lodged within my now-dry kelp bands. It had clearly held import for him, kept, as it was, hidden against his breast. I suspect this was another of the flares the woman-thing worried over.

I knew what I must do.

Sliding back down the outcrop, harsh rock scraping free dried scales as I went, I slipped with a grateful sigh back into the sea. Powerful twitches of my tail sent me around the rocks to where the two I'd watched still clung. From this new vantage point, I could see they perched because they could not climb higher against the algae-coated rock. This I could fix. The night air splintered with their shrieks as I braced against their bottoms, first the boy-thing, then the woman-thing, and with powerful thrusts of my tail surged forward, propelling them from the sea and up onto the rocks. They scrambled higher, clutching each other in as tight a grip as I'd held their man-thing when I drew him under the sea. I bobbed there where they had clung, merely watching, bemused but content that the waters would not have them. I met the gaze of the woman-thing, remorse in my eyes, though my tongue remained silent.

I had not the words to make my deed right, none to excuse them. I bowed my head down as I slid my hand into the kelp band, working the object free. It glowed in the moonlight as I brought it forth, and a gleam of hope lightened the terror in the woman-thing's expression. Like a crab, she sidled toward my outstretched hand, snatching my prize and scurrying back.

Without a word, I turned away and dropped beneath the waves, but not before I glanced a fleeting moment up into the sky. Someday I would dance with the lightning and climb its jagged bolts into the heavens. Someday... I would reach those distant shores to swim the seas of the unseen moon.

But not today.

Previously published in *Mermaid 13*, Padwolf Publishing.

ON THE WINGS OF AN ANGEL

Can't say as I didn't reckon I was going mad. It wouldn't have surprised me if'n it was so. I already reckoned I was in hell. That's enough to turn anyone's mind...

But first, I call myself Miss Sadie Angelina Carlisle, though I don't bother much with any name but the middle one anymore. Not since takin' up residence at the Lucky Strike Saloon in Dead Dog, Montana, anyway. See, the proprietor, Mr. Clayton, he says men are happier pretendin' they're keepin' company with an angel, rather than a common whore. I do as I'm told, else Mr. Clayton might forget he likes havin' an angel below stairs temptin' and teasin' the custom, rather than just another girl entertainin' above stairs. Men don't pay near so much for common. They have to save up for an angel, even a fallen one, unless they hit a strike. That ain't happened yet. Till then, I sing.

"Sadie! Sun's settin', quit wool-gatherin', and get yourself into your rig afore I find someone else as fits it!"

Lordie, but that black-hearted Clayton can bellow. I can't help but shudder at his bald-faced threat, though. That happens, and I might as well drop the name Angel too. Ain't none of us outta reach of his temper. I'd do to remember that. And I reckon he's been givin' me looks makin' me wonder will I be below stairs much longer anyhow. Looks that make me think he's tired of waitin' for a prospector with that big strike to come along. I've no doubt I've only been spared entertainin' the custom 'cause there ain't anyone come in able to pay the price Mr. Clayton has set on my innocence.

I flinch at the thought and rush to do as I'm bid, my mind near jibberin' half-formed pleas for deliverance, but not hardly expectin' it will ever come. I'm already wearin' my white satin gown and matchin' slippers with the thick leather soles; now for the rest. Quick-like, I beckon over Shelby, one of the above stairs ladies, for some help 'cause I plum can't suit up all myself.

See, our Mr. Clayton, he's into mods and mechanicals. Show him somethin' with gears, and I reckon he starts breathin' like he's been with a five-dollar whore. There are bits of invention all over the saloon I can scarce make sense of. They're most nothin' much but tinker's toys like the little metal birds what can't fly, but sing pertier than me... if'n only ever just one song, and miniature carriages made for Cook's son movin' by themselves on tiny puffs of steam... The bartender is flesh enough, but there ain't a bottle of liquor to be seen—nor broke, if'n the custom gets rowdy. Drinks is portioned out by a clockwork contraption of gears and pipes that can take a dent and keep on pourin' the next drink in just as precise a measure as the last. Then there's the player piano what plays itself like any other, but ain't no crank involved, just lotsa steam and valves and whatnot. It's an amazin' thing of copper and brass instead of wood, with gold-plated keys, and not soundin' no more tinny than any other upright I ever heard.

But all of that ain't nothin' compared to my rig.

I can't help but think about that with longin' and loathin' mixed, rememberin' when and how it came to be. There was a tinker come through town. An odd, dirt-smudged, little man what made me more nervous than an uncooped hen after dark. The first he scurried into the saloon and looked his fill at every one of us, we felt near stripped bare down to our very souls, though there weren't nothin' to it that was lecherous or mean. More like Mr. Edward S. Curtis, what came through with his pho-tography equipment once on his way to visit the Blackfoot injuns; he used to look just so at near everythin' like he was searchin' for the perfect picture it would make.

I swear if I didn't feel the tinker's gaze linger just the same on me, though I can't fathom why. I was a young'n yet at the time, and nothin' special to catch the custom's eye. Like now, I sang for my place when I weren't cleanin'.

Was the tinker first called me Angel, with a nervous-makin' gleam in his eye—like he saw more to me than I right knew was there—and him not even knowin' my given name. That amused Mr. Clayton so much it stuck.

Then that there tinker set to catch Mr. Clayton's attention with such contraptions as you can't never imagine and I can scarce describe. The things that came out of his sack... my Lord, it was a sight. The two of 'em spent more'n a piece of time with their heads together, hagglin'. Hard to say who hoodwinked who, but both men walked away with a smarmy smile.

The tinker stayed a spell after. He puttered around in the cellar until near all you heard afore hours was bangin' and the hiss of steam, but evenin's he ended up in the saloon pesterin' me. Askin' questions and starin' me up and down mutterin' "not yet" under his breath, like maybe I didn't quite match the picture in his head.

The questions made me more nervous than the mutterin'. They was dangerous questions: *What did I wish for? What would I rather be?* I was too feared then to speak, but my heart... it was cryin' out to be free! There was nothin' I wanted more than deliverance. The tinker just nodded and gave me a wink, like he heard what I ain't said, before disappearin' again back down to the cellar.

I wanted to believe. Darn near convinced myself he could do anythin'—includin' save me—after seein' him tinker with one of the songbirds what always sang particularly sad. I'd felt my forehead for a fever when he closed up its tiny back and brushed a finger over it what set it glitterin' and glowin' like pixie dust. Then... that little bird took wing, flyin' out the window never again to be seen! It trilled a happy song as it escaped.

A *different* song.

That's when I had to wonder was I goin' mad.

And still, I took to hopin' then, though ain't nothin' ever come of it.

Afore he left for good, that little man cornered me in the pantry whiles I was helpin' Cook with supper. He stood there, hunched and taut, again starin' me up and down all familiar-like. "Don't you worry... for now, you're safer here," he'd murmured, his head side-cocked, and his eyes narrowed like he was lookin' again for his own perfect picture. "But remember, when that's no longer so... Angels were made to fly."

His words left me ashiver in a way I declare I'd never felt afore or since.

To this day, I can hear him whisperin' that, and would swear on my dead ma's Bible if'n I had it that I sometimes still spy him in the shadows, watchin', eyes narrowed just so, though I know he's gone. Quite mad, true, I but can't help but wishin' that mayhap the tinker was right, and I'll have me a chance to fly away.

Anyhow, by the time the tinker finally moved along after considerable time spent in the cellar, the parlor had acquired somethin' wondrous new.

Even now, I can't help but hold my breath whiles Shelby unlocks my special cabinet. The thing is tall, clear up to the above stairs ceilin'. The whole front and sides foldin' back with fancy paintin' everywhere on the inside, like you would imagine heaven to be, all but for what Mr. Clayton calls the new-matic tube; a brass pipe runnin' down the center, shiny as the day the tinker set it in place.

My rig just hangs there in the middle of the air like someone forgot to paint in the angel, 'ceptin' for its halo and wings—I ain't ever yet been tall enough for that halo to perch proper atop my head. Each time I see The Angel, it dazzles me, so's I always near forget how much I dread to buckle the contraption on.

Ain't got no choice, though. Never did. Mr. Clayton says an Angel's gotta have wings if'n anyone's gonna believe she fell from heaven.

An' mayhap they do, when I'm singin'—if I can be forgiven the smallest bit of pride. Savin' for my voice, there's precious little about me that ain't common, or so my pa used to say. 'Course, given this rig here—and the presence of the above stairs ladies— I'd be a mite surprised did the gents notice a thing about myself, no matter that I'm hoverin' in thin air above their heads lookin' near the picture of angelic. (Times like that, I can't help but remember the tinker's words... and that little metal songbird. My heart goes all tight each time I do...)

Oh glory, just to look at it... Wings made of gen-u-ine swan feathers brushed light like with gold. Mr. Clayton's after callin' it *guilt*, then laughin' his fool ass off like'n he said somethin' funny. Which, given the nature of his establishment...

I'm mighty fond of those perty wings. The corset, though... that there's a pure torment to wear. I must stand just so the entire time if'n I'm to have enough air to breathe, let alone sing as I'm expected. I do imagine were not the whole thing latched on to the new-matic tube I *could* plum fly away. I reckon I wish that were so somethin' fierce.

Right now, the only things protectin' my virtue is my singin' and my not-quite-generous curves. I'm afeared that won't be so for long bein' I've had to dodge more'n a few grabbin' hands of late.

Before Mr. Clayton can bellow once more, I step up onto the platform makin' up the bottom of the cabinet, and though I mostly feel forsaken, I lift up a prayer to the God my ma once swore by. After all, in a manner, she'd been delivered, even if her passin' had left me to bear pa alone, if'n only for a short spell, before he foisted me off on Mr. Clayton.

I step into the frame, careful of the many danglin' straps and buckles, makin' sure my feet set just so on the narrow brass plate they're meant to perch on. I shudder to recall the time they'd slipped from that square. The breath was near squeezed out of me. I've learned to be particular since. My eyes close all on their own, and I draw deep and full till my lungs near want to burst as Shelby cages me in that rig of iron ribbin', white leather, and polished brass. Otherwise, there ain't no room to breathe once the contraption's buckled tight.

Those lookin' on see nothin' but perty; from the moment I'm buckled in till they free me, I'm nigh in pain, forced to stand straight and still as Sundy service else scald my back on the gleamin' brass pole behind me.

It was a wonder I could ever sing a note, but derned if I don't put the nightingale to shame each and every night when I put on The Angel and dangle there in 'heaven' to give the custom a show, and that ain't no boast.

I hear the clunk of the lever bein' pulled across the room, followed by the hiss of steam warmin' the ledge beneath my feet. There's the *whir* of shiftin' gears as the wings spread, and I feel just a bit giddy as I rise up in the air above the platform. Can't help but wonder maybe this time I won't stop in the middle. Mayhap I'll be crushed against the ccilin' or, mayhap, I'll sure enough fly away. There ain't no holdin' back my giggle at that. But then the sound of the hiss changes and my perch slows, then stops.

I feel it then. A shiver down m'spine. Familiar-like, enough that I expect I'd see him... the tinker... if'n my eyes weren't shut. I imagine I hear that little songbird as well, and I let my eyes drift open to see did either of 'em really come back.

But all that's there is the familiar sight of The Angel framed in the mirror behind the bar. Only not quite the same as always...

Just a tiny gasp escapes me, and I forget to look for what I expected.

For the first time ever, that there halo's just behind my head and The Angel's starin' back, all brown-gold curls and creamy white skin, with a tiny waist and a bosom to put the above stairs ladies to shame. She's wearin' my face.

But it ain't that what startles me. It were Mr. Clayton holdin' up a walnut-sized nugget of gold with a shit-eatin' grin on his face. Standin' next to him was a grubby, overlarge miner smellin' rank even from here.

No longer able to deny my days of bein' safe were done, I recoil, only to have fierce heat sear my back.

I don't smell scorched satin or burnt flesh, as I'd expect. I smell a garden like my ma use to have, and again I hear that tiny metal bird. The burnin's gone afore I even draw breath to cry out, and in the mirror I swear that pipin' hot brass ain't at my back no more.

A gasp rises from every throat in the room, and if I weren't so scared, I'd laugh as their eyes go wide, but I'm afraid to move, afraid to fall. Then somethin' brushes my shoulders, sends them tinglin' like they been long asleep and only just wakin' up. I start to glitter. I shiver again, and a flush steals over me. Wisps of steam curl at my feet like soft white clouds, no longer over warm. Then... quiet by my ear, barely louder'n a breath... I hear the tinker's sigh-like whisper, "Now... be free."

I feel like I imagine that bird did, afraid to believe... afraid not to.

My body shakes at the tinker's words, eager like tremors from head to toe. Mayhap I imagine it... mayhap I truly am mad... but somethin' sparks off my skin, rises up from my bones, and sets me aglow. I remember the songbird as I feel the sudden flex of wings at my back, the bunchin' of muscles I ain't ever used. I open my mouth and out pours a terrible, wonderful, glorious sound.

As The Angel sings, the buckles fall away, and m'iron cage rains to the sawdust-covered floor in pieces as gilded feathers lift me to the sky.

Previously published in *In An Iron Cage: The Magic of Steampunk,* Dark Quest Books.

CROSSROADS AND CURSES

"NEVER PISS OFF A WITCH."

Sound advice... not what I'd expected, but sound just the same—even for someone like me with no belief in witches.

"No need to smirk, human," the elvin warrior grumbled.

I was pretty sure I wasn't but didn't argue. That might piss *him* off and then all of this would have been for nothing. Instead, I examined him closely. If the season were closer to All Hallow's Eve I would expect I was being had. How else to explain a seven-foot-tall, ancient-seeming warrior suddenly sprawled across a rough, old bench in the middle of nowhere?

Only this was Beltane by the pagan calendar, and I'd told no one what I'd intended. Over weeks and months, I had gathered those items I'd felt I would need to ensure success. Not one thing I'd brought or worn had been manufactured by modern means, there was no steel or iron anywhere on me, and the burlap sack at my feet contained every protective or ritual object I could possibly need gleaned from the collective legends of the crossroads: twenty-one pennies, three candies; a hazel switch broom; garlic, even a battered violin, and the list went on.

I hadn't needed any of them. Dude must have been bored.

I would swear I'd never seen him before, yet something about him echoed familiar on a subconscious level. With a reporter's trained eye, I took mental note of his long, narrow features. His tabard—worn over a heavy tunic and woven leather leggings—bore some symbol I did not recognize woven through with what appeared to be thread-of-gold. Have to admit, I coveted the boots on his feet, but I raised my eyebrow at the sheathed steel at his hip. Proof he was fake? Possibly. Possibly not. There was some debate on the issue of iron and the fae.

Other than the symbol, which I quickly sketched upon the parchment stretched across my knees, I committed his features to memory, not skilled enough with my borrowed quill to waste time and effort on secondary details. As the sharpened tip scratched across the surface, the warrior glared at me with silver-gilt eyes from beneath ebon locks that would have had any number of runway divas wanting to pull it out of jealousy. The delicate, curved point of an ear poked through as well. Either this guy was the real deal, or he was a nutjob with theatrical training. Neither possibility was quite comfortable, but I'd endured worse when on a story.

I pushed strands of ordinary brown hair out of the way behind my own ear to better see by the light of the beeswax candle held in place on the bench between us by its own drippings. Surprisingly, no fragrance rose from it. And another peculiar thing... other than the bit I'd melted to keep the whole thing standing upright, the taper hadn't burned down. The flame remained steady and bright in the surrounding darkness.

The elf cleared his throat, his impatience somehow sounding elegant, dignified. It was startling as the night was unnaturally silent, with not a trill from the night birds or chirp from a cricket. The look in his eye had grown no less intent, but had taken on a puzzled air. He almost looked put out. "But *why* are you here?"

Here was a defunct bus stop at a country crossroad.

"I want to know the truth," I answered.

"The truth is a stone-cold bitch."

Wow. How raw... and crude. So at odds with the outward image; I was leaning a bit more toward him being a nutjob, but I had to be sure.

"Let's start small," I said. "The candle, why doesn't it burn down?"

"We are in Midnight."

My eyes darted to my wrist, seeking a watch that was not there. I'd been sitting here too long for it to still be midnight. "I don't understand..."

"Not midnight... *Midnight*," he answered, as if I were slow. "Some things are immutable; when you enter a crossroads at the precise moment of midnight you overlap the realm of Midnight, a place where there is no time... no boundary, only expectation. Everywhere at once and nowhere at all."

I laughed. Okay, suspicion confirmed. Nutjob.

I had a feeling I was wasting my time. I should have known by now that the truth we look for isn't always the one we find. A childhood memory had led me to this place. It was old, thin, and faded, but cherished. To be expected. I was only three years old when it happened. My family had gone camping, and I'd wandered off. I was lost, alone, and frightened. It was the middle of the night at a crossroad that felt very much the same as where I found myself now. I'd cried for the knight from my picture book to save me and he had come. The next morning I'd woken up safe beside my mother with the memory already fading. Like one of my faerie tales, only I'd been so sure it was real. I *needed* to know if it was real. Gee... which one of us was delusional again?

Not wanting to think about that too hard, I fired off a question of my own: "Why are *you* here?"

This time he laughed. Rich and bold and, again, somehow familiar.

"Me?" he asked. "*I* pissed off a witch."

He laughed again and I huffed out a sigh, tired of cryptic and tired of feeling like the only one who didn't get the joke. Leaving the candle where it was and setting aside the parchment and quill, I started to reach down for my bag, halting with a shiver at a change in the air. I looked up, confused, only to be thrust to the ground. The scrape of drawn steel made my gut clench and sent me rolling beneath the weathered bench before the thought was complete. I waited for the sound of steel biting wood, or worse, flesh.

It did not come.

I peered up through the slats expecting to meet his crazed molten-silver gaze. What I saw was Elvin Warrior Dude faced off with some gawky SCA escapee. Pot-metal against Toledo steel. It was like something out of a movie; the formal challenge, the flourished salute, the nearly choreographed engagement. Well, half of the exchange anyway. Sir Gawkwin moved more like a trained bear... plenty of enthusiasm... not much grace. Slash.

Jab. Clanging metal. Ringing steel. Grunts and sweat and sparks flew out from the center of the crossroad. The air carried the sharp aroma of blood.

I flinched but could not look away—though with the evidence at eye-level, part of my thoughts absently took note that still my candle did not drip, did not burn down. And then beyond all belief shining steel was struck from elvin hand and pot-metal point came to rest upon the tabard where it met smooth, pearly skin. At the tip welled a perfect ruby drop.

"Yield!" the kid half-squeaked and half-growled.

My mouth fell open as the elf went to his knees, head bowed.

I wanted to yell, to scream, to take up the sword sticking in the ground not two feet away and kick the pimply geek's ass. (Remember... delusional.) But I could only watch with fascination as the kid's expression transformed and boy became man. The cheap blade was lowered, and a more subdued salute sketched, then the guy walked away, bloodied, but unbowed.

Tension pounded a tempo against my skull. Snippets of recalled research came to mind... Hectate, Legba, vampires and ghosts and faeries... but I could scarcely reconcile them with what I'd witnessed. I closed my eyes and sought a moment of reason in the aftermath of chaos. I so wanted to believe what had transpired was a hoax, but I could not.

A weight settled on the bench while I was failing to find my zen. He made no sound, but for lightly labored breathing, which quickly steadied. I opened my eyes and glanced at him through the slats, finding myself closer to a bloodied gaping thigh than I cared to be.

"What... the hell... was that?" I managed, my voice coming out thin and my breath smelling faintly of panic.

"What he expected," was the weary answer.

I crept out from my shelter and put a bit of distance between us. Should have paid attention; I ended up between him and his sword. A good thing? A bad thing? It could go either way.

Elvin Warrior Dude sighed. Shook his head. Gave me a look that said, 'come on already.' Then he ran his hands across the rents in his clothing and over his angry wounds. I gasped and my eyes went wide. If the scent of blood weren't still in my nose I would have wondered was I going mad. His hands began to glow, and as they passed over the damage it faded swiftly away.

"I am, and have ever been," he said, "the guardian of the four-armed crossroads. In my prideful and foolish youth, I forgot that honor bore responsibility. Hectate has seen fit to remind me. The mortal world has been seeded with legends that I must oblige."

I must have still looked confused.

"You came here seeking truth?" It was a question, but not. I nodded anyway. "That boy came desiring to prove himself in a faerie challenge."

"This is your truth: I am perceived as all things as needed… To those who believe and enter the crossroads I must be whatever they seek." Again, I thought of my research, and trembled.

"Hardly anyone comes looking for a hero," he said as if my thoughts were open to him.

And before my eyes the elvin warrior shimmered. For only a moment I caught a glimpse of the shining knight of my childhood before he sketched a salute and faded gently away.

Somewhere a cricket chirped. Only then did the scent of melting beeswax finally waft on the air.

Previously published in *The Fox's Fire,* Paper Phoenix Press.

PORTRAIT OF
A GREEN MOTHER

A ravaged beauty
cloaked in a patchwork mockery
of her former splendor
a crown of timeless flowers
woven in what's left her hair
with one hand she cradles humanity
the other fends off society's blows

MOON DANCE

THE MOON DANCED IN STATELY, SOLITARY STEPS. DRIPPING FROM her full, round curves, moonbeams spiraled down to kiss all below. The swirls of faint light only served to accentuate the darkness. Crickets kept the tempo and I... I provided the melody. Silver strings rippled beneath my fingers. I knew how they felt. The very music they cried forth sent tingles down my spine and silent tears down my cheeks. I hid them behind the curtain of my silver-gilt hair. I did not wish to be there. Were I able, I would flee. Yet my fingers played on.

A hand came down heavy upon my shoulder as the Moon set. The notes faltered, and the harp went silent. My numb fingers fell away while the rest of me remained taut, unmoving, wary...

"What did she whisper?"

I squeezed my eyes tight and fought to find the words... Fought to keep them secret... Fought to not cry out, rather than answer. The conflict allowed a shudder to escape my rigid controls.

My tormentor's hand tightened and he laughed. Harsh and cruel and hard, the sound weighed heavier upon me than anything else that night.

"What?" The fingers dug into my flesh as he lost his patience.

"The first speaks of conquest, the second treachery. You will face both before the Moon again forsakes the sky...

"From the steppes, the Shadowcat draws nigh, its teeth sheathed in a lambkin's flesh. He paces the edges of his land, restless and hungry, always hungry." I shivered despite the warmth of the night air. The omen frightened me nearly as much as the man standing at my back. The thought was not comfortable. I did not know what to wish for: victory or defeat from the envisioned menace.

"Continue!" my master growled, low and threatening.

I flinched. I could not help it, and I cursed myself. I'd fallen silent for too long. In his annoyance, he shook me hard. My forehead slammed against the frame of the harp, and I whimpered before I could stop, afraid not for myself, but for the precious instrument. It was the last of my legacy, all else had been stripped from me, destroyed before my eyes. My tormentor laughed again as I bit back an agonized moan.

"From out of the desert, one whirlwind sweeps into the path of another in Boroki City... when they meet, unfortunates will pick up the fragments of their lives from the rubble, but none will blame the forces of nature." I kept my voice flat, unfeeling. In my heart, I cursed him. "Fault lies with the wind that blew them, not themselves.

"The Moon Maiden speaks of nothing more."

"What nonsense," he sneered. I could not see it, but I could hear it in the rise and fall of his words. "What does it mean? And why should I care?"

Long ago, I had learned that it was not enough to eavesdrop on the Moon. I must translate accurately, or I would be the one blood-red by the end of the night. The battle I fought within was ongoing. It sickened me to help him in any way, but I must survive to one day be free. Besides, he would learn of this, whether I spoke or not. He had spies that delivered willingly, if not as prompt.

Finally, I spoke slowly, with care. "To the east are the Banakar Steppes. Among the tribes roaming there, a man has risen to unrivaled power. He moves like a panther and is dark as eternal night, both in appearance and temperament. He seeks to found a dynastic rule. His eyes are set upon borders far beyond those he already claims. Those caught between him, and his goal will be slaughtered without remorse. His gaze and his interest sweep from shore to far shore."

"The Banakar Steppes? I have nothing to fear from wandering goat herders; my armies will crush them beneath steel-shod heels." With a flick of his fingers, he dismissed the omen. "And this other? What was it? The whirlwinds?"

The words dripped with amusement and disdain. I ignored his tone and continued.

"The desert has hidden its face for a generation. Two of its children, forced by circumstance, will find themselves in Boroki City. They will be the center of such turmoil that your subjects will be devastated. The root of the cause lies with an enemy you do not yet know you possess."

He fell silent. I could sense this last unsettled him. Treachery was ever foremost in his mind. And well it should be. If it were not for treachery, he—King Loaghnin—would yet be a general, and I—Queen Aurora of the eternal line of royal Xhan—would not be his slave, made to eavesdrop on her mother—the Moon.

GREEN WITH ENVY

I.

LOOK AT HIM... WENDING HIS WAY AROUND ROCKS AND DEADFALL, moving farther and farther away... pitiful, little bug. Her eyes flared green like new-minted leaves and her supple skin, as brown as a butternut, rippled and gleamed in the dappled sunshine streaming through Daire's crown. She slinked gracefully around the bole, climbing higher, keeping the walking stick in sight.

"Where are you going, twig?" she whispered in dulcimer tones laced with bitter chill. "What do you hope to find in your wanderings?"

With careful precision, placing each delicate stilt-like leg just so, the bug continued on, oblivious to the venom borne upon the air. Dangling from the upper branches like an erotic dream, she arched and twisted, clinging to limbs that by all rights should have bowed and snapped at even her slight weight. A whimsical wind tugged at her leaf-tangled tresses and dragged upon her frame, half-heartedly trying to unseat her grip.

The dryad seethed and burned at the futility. As if she wouldn't cast herself to the ground with a moment's chance. As if she wouldn't descend from her towering branches to feel the dirt firsthand between her toes. Once again her gaze settled on the oblivious and taunting stick bug, shrinking into the distance, wandering off into the wondrous world. He knew how it goaded her, tied to her tree as sure as if vines twisted around her naked flesh, her lack of freedom cutting and chaffing worse than physical bindings.

She threw her head back and cried amber tears as the leaves above gave voice to her weeping.

II.

THE WORLD WAS SO LARGE AROUND HIM, SO DIFFICULT TO CONCEIVE. Every obstacle was a mountain and every breeze a gale. Slowly he made his way, leaving behind his greatest torment, his longing. Such beauty... such power... such disregard...

Didn't she know the value of her roots? Didn't she realize the an-choring security to be found cradled in the limbs of the mighty oak? She shunned her fortune even as he craved it. None could harm her, while his very nature required he hide wherever he went.

To set aside his vulnerability... to put behind him forever the need to freeze and cower in place at every cast shadow...

That would be heaven.

He sighed heavily and drew a slow, steady limb across his eyes. The stick bug could not bear to exist in her shadow a moment more; instead he braved the great unknown, where the effect of his camouflage was much diminished. He would find a new home with no spoiled dryad bemoaning her fate. With grim determination he slowly crept over another rock, leaving at his back a trail of amber tears.

LEAVING IN THE SPRING

CLIMBING FROM THE DARKNESS, HALF-CONSCIOUSLY GRUMBLING AS the growing warmth of the morning sun took the chill off her slum-bering limbs, Daire could feel liquid fire running through her veins. Standing naked and tall in the dew-bejeweled grass of her sheltered valley, her slight and graceful frame swayed with the gentle breezes that danced around her.

The sunshine was gloriously warm after the cold, distant light of winter. Spring was here and Daire and her young sisters felt an over-whelming hunger for the life-giving rays that beat down upon them. Though their thoughts were still muddled with sleep, each of them in-stinctively strained against their own skin, discontent with waiting for the caress of the golden sun to reach for them, wanting only to rush forward to meet it. The tips of their swaying, sun-warmed limbs trembled as the liquid fire pulsed through them.

And still they craved more. Every ounce of their will focused on embracing the brilliant light, clasping it to them like a lover whose ab-sence had lasted exceedingly long. No, more like children reaching out for a parent who had been sorely missed. And still their efforts were not enough. Pressing even harder against their overly tight skin, they yearned for relief, feeling close to bursting. With a final bittersweet agony and a glorious flutter of new-minted green, they gathered in the sunlight, their newly unfurled leaves dancing merrily in the vernal breeze.

Winter was gone and, for the oaks of the valley, Spring was the season for leaving.

TRUE TO FORM

last night i dreamt of fuchsia cloud
i wish my soul could hear the song
of the wild leafy sea dragons
soaring among the aerial waves

i wish my soul could hear the song
made savory with the salt of evaporated tears
soaring among the aerial waves
the heart of humanity in vibrant bleeding colors

made savory with the salt of evaporated tears
my memories of love color my perception
the heart of humanity in vibrant bleeding colors
reflects for me the haunting image of your retreating back

my memories of love color my perception

ODD JASON OUT

pan flutes titillate the ear
leading his thoughts
a merry chase
through decadence

an artful glimpse
of curve at breast and thigh
through tousled tresses
as shapely legs
dance to the piper
in wooded glade

fluttering hands
graceful as a butterfly
beckon a siren's call
as ancient eyes burn
with unfettered passion

unuttered
yet clearly written
in arched brow
and hints of a smile
tugging tempting lips
there is no sin
in natural order

but society is
an unnatural child

SYLVAN GLADE

THE SKY WAS FADED WHITE AND SULTRY, THE FLOWERS WILTING beneath the heavy weight of sunbeams unmitigated by any hint of breeze. Nothing cut through the heated torment of August... not sound nor shade nor movement of any kind. Every creature hid, fleeing the ominous atmosphere of the dog day.

In the folds formed of limp cabbage leaves tented over the cracked soil, a gecko spied a flutter of gossamer, languid and futile in the effort to draw some cooler air. Could that little nook afford more comfort than the meager shade offered by his baking rock? The lizard scampered closer, streaking toward the haven, imagining cool, dark earth and the moist scent of green. He would oust the little insect and have the space for his own. So riveting was his daydream, he had no thought of the path behind him, or what might be lurking there.

There was no sound or warning, foreboding was indistinguishable from the oppressive atmosphere of noon. As the gecko wended his way beneath the shelter of his goal, reality erupted into snarls and floating fur, shredded cabbage leaves and churned earth. The gecko became a red smear, his blood feeding the parched soil even as his flesh fed the cat.

With an irritated flurry of blinding white wings, the moth took to the air in search of sanctuary elsewhere.

IMAGINE THAT

Dream for a moment
Picture her languid beauty
Worship frantically
A soaring goddess
Then wake with her magic
Glimmering in your eye
Revealing to you
Like faery water
The wonders of the world
Hidden from mortal sight
Fae-touched minstrel
Play us your songs
Of immortal splendor
Color our perception
With Titania's mystique
Freeing us
If but a moment
From the mundane shades
Of life's demands
And wrap us in
In brilliant, rainbow hues
With the power
To grant us our dreams

DESERT DANCER

K Y'A WAS NEARLY SPENT, UTTERLY WORN AWAY BY THE UNRELENTING wind, scoured by the sand one moment, and shriveled by the sun the next. Her maimed body would have stretched upon the dunes long ago if not for her pride. She was one of the Kylo'tha... the Desert Dancers. The honorific had nothing to do with music or dancing, unless one counted the melody of their fierce cries or the fluid, graceful moves with which they cheated death upon the desert sands.

She had stumbled in the Dance. She bore the scars on her flesh and upon her honor. She had been stripped as was the custom of her people and sent into the desert to find her redemption. She would find death, or a miracle, but she would never again find her way home.

The oasis behind her had blessed her with water for her hardened throat and shade against the unrelenting sun, but the hearts of the palm that were a staple of the Kylo'than diet had all been harvested. The end was drawing near and it seemed the desert would conquer her at last. Her belly grew heavy in its emptiness, drawing her into a cramped hunch. Heat danced off the desert in mockery and Ky'a, for the first time in her banishment, felt despair. Death visions formed upon the vapors.

By'al, the Sun's blazing white stallion and bearer of the dead, was coming for her. Even now she could hear his battle screams as she tumbled to the ground. Her heart screamed back in triumph. She had found redemption; what approached was a warrior's death. The dull rumble of granite hooves upon the sands echoed in her ears. Ky'a looked up, baring her throat to her god's messenger, bracing herself for his tearing teeth.

They did not strike.

Dishonor then. By'al was to be her judge and not her deliverer. Ky'a's stomach rumbled and her eyes closed in her disgrace. Soon the hunger would mean nothing to her. The honored died by By'al's teeth, the disgraced died beneath his hooves.

Still, death did not descend.

With wondering eyes, Ky'a looked up and nearly laughed. This was not white By'al, but her own Ky'il of the palest silver-grey only the ignorant called white. The sun glowed like a benediction off his hide, but the shredded end of his halter was testament to his disgrace. He had escaped to rescue her. Again her stomach rumbled and, as she looked at her devoted stallion, the irreverent thought occurred to her that she would never be *that* hungry.

LUNA

Pale white sister
Against a faded blue sky
Resignedly watching
As your golden brother
Steals your glory
You quietly back away
From his gaudy, glaring brilliance
Timid in your own perfection

HORROR

RUBY RED

THERE WAS BLOOD ON THE COUNTER. JUST THREE LITTLE DROPS, bright and deep all at once. Startling against the white marble. I ran my finger through one gleaming half-globe. It smeared a red spectrum along the edge of the sink.

I giggled. The sound startled me. It was out of place in the surrounding starkness, slashing a hole in the silence that closed instantly. I was being disrespectful. Dragging my lower lip between my teeth, I reached for the roll of tissue and tore off a couple of squares. With great care, I wiped away the smear I'd made, leaving the remaining two drops pristine and the rest of the counter nothing but white. I balled the tissue and clutched it tight in my fist.

The urge to giggle swept through me once more, and I ground down harder on my lip. The pain was sharp and focusing. It allowed me to fight back the urge. It had been so long since I'd been allowed color. They didn't trust me with color. Things happened.

I wrapped my arms tight around my body and stared at the remaining two drops. Lost myself in the play of light upon the gleaming surfaces. They sparkled like gems. My breath quickened, and I had to tuck my hands beneath my arms to keep them still, to keep them from reaching out and playing with the pretty color.

"Red," I whispered. It was no more than a breath, nearly just a thought. I didn't want anyone to hear. They would take the drops away. "Red... red like rubies, like poppies under the sun, strawberries dripping with dew."

The intensity ran like a wire up my spine. Each word drew it taut; each image sprang into my mind and spawned more. I buried my senses in each thing that surfaced. My eyes were dazzled by the glimmer of jewels, my nose filled with the smell of warm flowers, my tongue savored the sweetness of ripe fruit.

"Red!"

The bathroom became a sea of red as my mental images shaped reality. Flower petals scattered over the cold, white tile; ripe fruit crushed beneath my feet as I circled the room. Power swirled around me, brushed my skin, danced among the strands of my hair. It was red as well. Everything was red.

I laughed with the joy of color. The white was swept away. Bending, I scooped my hands through the redness and encountered sharp-edge gems. I'd found my rubies. The sting of pain was life and I laughed more. Gone was the sterile white. I lifted my arms, pale, white skin trailing beads of blood from a hundred little nicks.

"Red! Red like blood!"

The bite of iron overwhelmed my other senses: the smell, the taste, the slick, thick feel of it against my skin. A liquid red tide swept over me, coating the walls and sweeping away fruit and flowers and gems.

"Red... red like blood," I whispered again, a mere moving of the lips, drowned out by the pulse of the tide.

Red swept me away.

Previously published in Trails of Indiscretion, Issue #1, Spring 2006; Fortress Publishing, Harrisburg, PA.

THE SILVERS

I saw Silvers down below today.
Posing as art.
Frozen in tableau.
Motionless, looking past the crowd at nothing.
Nothing is all they miss.
I used to want to be a Silver.
Before I knew better.
Now all I want to be is nothing.
I always run into them in the subway.
In the evening.
When everyone is too harried,
too weary to see them for what they are.
I am not everyone.
My link with society is loose at best.
I work very hard at not being
what they are looking for.
I hide beneath grime.
Beneath filth.
Beneath festering scabs.
I hide and I watch for them.
Those on their pedestals are easy to spy.
The identifiable threat.
I must watch for those that have found
what they are looking for.
A skin to slip inside.
A place to hide in the open
Unsuspected.

INNOCENCE

Sitting in a cloud of unrealized tears, blonde head bowed beneath the weight of wearying thoughts, a child's glazed eyes stared down the darkness. Strange her world had become in this new city, enough that it was easier to slip into dreams than to contemplate the nightmare.

In her dreams this filthy room was a starry meadow. Graceful willows lined the stream and field mice scurried beneath autumn leaves. It was a landscape she knew well from another life, one where she'd been kept safe by her brother's presence as the two of them braved the night. In that long-ago time, the shadows above them belonged to protective oaks, not decrepit buildings, and great snowy owls glided through the inky sky, her vigilant guardians.

But this was not a dream—the stars she saw peered through a fragmented roof, and the snowy owls in truth were nasty, dirty pigeons. The scurrying she heard were filthy rats rummaging among the news-papers for scraps. And her brother... a bag woman filled his role in reality, at least most nights.

She wondered where the old woman had gone. As a muttering shadow on the far side of the room, she had been nice, in a paranoid sort of way—never coming close, but still there. In her way she had even been generous, pelting the girl with bits of stale bread; a twisted attempt at sharing. The crusts were still on the floor; the child hadn't been hungry. To tell the truth, she couldn't remember what the feeling was like.

In total apathy, the child rolled over and stared at the sky, drifting into her mindless stupor. In the moonlight her chin was black with blood and no breath did flutter in her chest, but still above her head was a halo of unrealized tears. She rolled over, contemplating rats.

BURNING CONVICTION

ULTRAFINE. INSIDIOUS. SOFTLY SUFFOCATING. CLINGING DUST COATED the cavernous chamber and everything in it. It rose in swirling puffs with each step I took. I rubbed my fingertips together and flinched. The dust clung in persistent defiance of any efforts to slough it off. The powder mocked me with a phantom glide of natural oil that spoke of past incarnations. Sweat beaded on my forehead and streamed into my eyes. More trickled between my breasts and down the rest of me. It mingled with the dust that permeated everything I was wearing. Soon I would resemble the troll-like men moving about the chamber. They were coated in a thick grey crust that cracked, but never seemed to fall away.

Across the room an entire wall of massive convection ovens roared. As I moved closer, the infernal heat drew everything from the air—dust... humidity... oxygen. I opened my mouth to suck in what was to be had. The air scorched my lungs. The heat stole my body's moisture as I choked on dust.

"Someone get this fuckin' log outa my way until I'm ready for it!"

I tensed as the troll shoved past me.

"Stack it over with the others... now!"

I cocked an eye in the direction he gestured to with his thick, knobby chin. Piled longwise in the shadows were disturbingly familiar bundles, each between five and six feet long. Black bound in a fabric that glimmered with a dull sheen, there was a rough symmetry to them—small and rounded at the top, then doubling in thickness, until they tapered to a blunt point—but no two were exact in length or size. I quickly turned away. My jaw clenched and I swallowed hard against the sensation tightening my throat. A snarl twitched my lips. I lunged forward.

"Move me yourself, you ugly fucker!" I screamed back at him. "Who are you calling a..." An explosive pop sounded from the oven, cutting me off. White-hot flames shot out the opening.

The man didn't even look at me. He gave no sign that he heard my words. Instead, troll boy yelled and cursed and hurried toward the gapping maul of the blazing oven. Granite arms came around my chest and another set caught up my legs. I struggled and fought like a demon, screaming and cursing to rival the man in charge. He continued to ignore me as he grabbed a massive, charred paddle from the corner and slammed it into the fire. There was a loud crack, like bones breaking, and the sound of steam escaping. It rose with the eerie cadence of a keen. I shivered at the suffering in that sound; fell still and silent at the disturbing look on the man's face as he slid the paddle beneath the mound he'd just pummeled and flipped the mass over within the flame. A piece fell free.

I went limp in the grip of those carrying me. Tremors shook my body and my stomach heaved as I stared at the black, gnarled lump that landed just at the edge of the flame. My mind shut down, refusing to recognize what it saw. But it was too late for denial: there before me lay a disembodied hand, black and frozen in a frantic, useless claw.

"Okay. I'm ready," he grunted, shoving the paddle aside.

Those hauling me toward the mound stopped, and instead moved me forward.

I felt the fire's heat upon my face and screamed.

Previously published in *The Kindly One,* Paper Phoenix Press.

NO LONGER DREAMS

In my troubled sleep I thrash—
sweat-soaked blankets and I entwined.

At my throat claws a ragg'd breath,
and deep and low, in fear I whine.

Wisps of fog obscure my view
and twist my thoughts with every breath.

Hurry on without a chance—
It matters not... there is no path.

The Whisperer, keeping pace,
does not relent but lengthens stride,

Sounds the cry that chills my blood,
that echoes 'round from every side.

Cannot tell from where he'll strike
It is a game he loves to play.

Tracks me by my stench of fear,
draws close to taunt, then falls away.

Waking from my tortured sleep,
relieved for now, the hunt is done.

Stretching muscles tense with fright,
and wearily I greet the sun.

Yet too soon have I relaxed—
I open eyes and choke on screams.

There before me, staring back
The Whisperer—No longer dreams.

UNCAST SHADOWS

WE ARE THE UNCAST SHADOWS. THE THOUGHTS YOU DARE NOT acknowledge, the dreams you dare not pursue, the fears and regrets of a thousand lifetimes. We are what you will not admit, what and you cannot elude. You feel us in your very marrow and cut at your skin as if we would seep out the wounds and leave you free. Do you feel alive? It's a lie.

You lose a little more of yourself each time you do.

"Go away. You aren't real, you don't exist!"

You'd like to think so, wouldn't you? It doesn't work that way. Look at us. Go on... look... Do you find us familiar? Disturbingly so, I'm sure. This is your face upon every one of us. The one you hide beneath the endless masks you show the world.

You will not look away! We have been disregarded long enough. We surround you, hem you in on every side until you can scarcely draw breath. That's right. Whimper. Pant. Piss yourself as you catch even a glimpse of what is inside of you. Of what we are. What do we care? Our noses are deadened to all but the ever-present stench of rot. Soured dreams, putrid thoughts, moral decay.

"This isn't happening. No... this isn't happening."

Isn't it? Place your hand on your chest. Feel the rapid-fire pulse. Feel the clammy clinging of the gown. The trembling of your flesh... Look at us! You will see. You will concede. We exist. We will not be ignored. Do you think that pounding on your skull will drown us out? We could whisper on but a breath and still it would echo in your head. We could scream at the top of your lungs and not another would hear. There is not a space inside you we do not fill. Nowhere to hide, nowhere to escape. Not within this skin.

Or perhaps that is the problem? It binds you too tight, locks you in the here-and-now, anchors you. Don't you think?

Shed it. Strip it away. Pick until it loosens. Peel until you are free of it. It's only patchwork anyway, beneath the surface, where none can see... It comes apart in pieces oh so easily. Come... we'll help you...

———————————————————

Previously published in *The Kindly One,* Paper Phoenix Press.

REALISM

LOVED LETTER

THERE IS NOTHING IN HELL. THE SILENCES ECHO OFF THE AIR AND numbness has become status quo. The darkness would wrap me in black velvet if I allowed myself to feel it. Instead, I gladly drift along in senselessness.

I used to care. The void would encompass me and rage would rise to do battle with it, pushing it back. Leaving me huddled, a tiny speck in a queen-sized bed, adrift in a sea of once-white satin... What a stupid thing rage is. Why would I want to be witness to the destruction of my life? Embracing self-awareness is a masochistic nightmare.

There is no more resistance; I welcome oblivion. It saves me from the agony waiting on the outside.

Outside... where the screams echo off of walls papered in tattered mock-brocade that was so glorious when you hung it one long year ago... Scraps remain beneath my nails, forgotten. Outside where every little agony slices through nerves worn thin and brittle... worn away by platitudes and condolences. Outside where a part of me frantically clutches at the threads of life brutally torn asunder... one half of a broken pair.

What need have I to contemplate endless days in the company of your posthumous citation? No... there is nothing in Hell... and I welcome its oblivion before the emptiness of a life without you.

BE-MUSED

Closing out the world
with one finger pressed
against my ear,
the whispers of my soul
dance around the edges
of the remaining,
half-heard rumble.
Tantalizing glimpses
of illusive inspiration
like a vaguely familiar face
lost in a crowd,
or Pegasus
hiding in the stars
the way wild mares
lose themselves
among the trees.
Creative genius thwarted
by the erratic chaos
of the human mind.

A PORTRAIT OF
BLACK VELVET

SITTING ALL DAY IN A HARD, STRAIGHT-BACKED CHAIR, TAMMY fidgeted as she absently stroked the soft, stiff skirt of her black velvet dress. Occasionally, big people she didn't know would look at her and shake their heads, looking just like the silly plastic dog in Daddy's car, with its head that bobbed around on a spring. It was hot and she was sleepy, so sleepy her eyes blurred. But she stubbornly looked around, determined to stay awake.

The room was full of chairs like hers, chairs and people and flowers. The people didn't interest her anymore, with their dark clothes, pale faces, and bobbing heads, they all looked alike. She was interested in the flowers though. Her Mommy loved flowers and so did she.

She couldn't see the front of the room, but there were so many flowers she could see some of them over the people's heads. They were so beautiful—so many different colors and shapes. She loved flowers. Not so sleepy anymore, she tried to pick out the ones she knew. They were so mushed together that she had to concentrate extra hard to tell them apart.

Still rubbing her skirt, Tammy played her new game. In the far corner of the room, in front of the old lady with hair the color of periwinkles, was a bunch of flowers every shade of yellow and orange. First she recognized the daffy dills, then the tiger lilies (a funny name for a flower with spots and not stripes) then there were golden mums, which they always picked for grandma because Mommy calls her "Mum", and there were the ruffly white flowers that looked dipped in yellow paint—she couldn't remember the name.

She wanted to see more flowers, but the big people were in the way. Tammy climbed up until she stood on the seat of her chair, her tiny hand clutching the back so she didn't fall. Satisfied with her new view, she continued her game, able to see so much more from up high.

Her eyes continued to move across the room and she silently named the blossoms she knew, making her way through roses and daisies and lots more of the ruffly flowers—car-nations... they were car-nations—until she noticed something odd; there in the middle of all the flowers was a big, beautiful box, all glowing wood and shiny gold, just like Mommy's jewelry box. All the big people got to go look in the box, or kneeled on the bar in front of it like in church. Tammy thought she would like to look in the box too. Maybe it had pretty things in it like Mommy had in hers. Some-times she sat with Mommy on her bed and went through all the sparkly jewelry, which made Tammy happy. But she thought maybe she didn't want to look in the box after all, because when the big people turned around their faces scrunched the way hers did when she was sad, like when Daddy or Mommy went away from her. She kind of felt like that right now as she watched the periwinkle lady cry. Everyone else still shook their heads at Tammy. She didn't like the way they looked at her.

Tammy was no longer interested in flowers; she looked at her skirt so she didn't have to see the sad faces. They made her want to cry too. Seeing her dress of black velvet and the purple-black stain on the hand that had rubbed it smooth, she thought of Mommy and wished she knew where she was. Mommy would be mad to see Tammy's dirty hands, but she would wash them and hug Tammy on her lap so she wouldn't have to see the big people try to smile while they cried, their heads bobbing.

Her Mommy made this dress. She made it just for Tammy, with pretty white lace on the bottom and arms, and white rib-bons and a sash. A tiny frown tugged at Tammy's lip. The lace and ribbons were gone, with tiny black threads left behind in their place. Daddy had said in a funny little voice that they had to; he said Mommy would understand. Tammy hoped so—she didn't want Mommy to be mad at her. She wanted Mommy now.

Looking around, Tammy tried to find her Mommy in the crowd. She couldn't find her.

Up by the box was her Daddy, slowly turning around. Moving stiff and slow, he looked so sad. She didn't like to see him sad. Carefully climbing down off the hard chair, she tried to go to him.

"Daddy?" Tammy's small voice wasn't even noticed in the hum of big-people voices. "Daddy? Where'd my Daddy go?"

Moving toward the big box where she'd seen him, Tammy's lips trembled with each step. She couldn't find Daddy now. No one noticed as she made her way to the front of the room. She reached the pretty box and still no Daddy. Climbing onto the padded bar in front, Tammy peered in, curious about what everyone was looking at. She was confused but happy. Tammy hadn't found Daddy, but there was Mommy, wearing her dress that she made to be just like Tammy's.

Why was everyone watching Mommy sleep? Tammy reached in to caress Mommy's black velvet skirt. She looked so pretty.

"Mommy?" Tammy's voice quavered, without her knowing why. "Mommy, wake up."

As Tammy rubbed the soft, stiff velvet of her Mommy's skirt, big arms closed around her and held her tight. Looking up, she saw Daddy's face, red and streaming with tears. He was shaking with silent sobs. Closing her own brimming eyes, Tammy continued to caress both black velvet dresses.

SCIENCE FICTION

FOREVER AND A DAY

*"A dream is a memory of what the future may hold
if you dare to reach for it."*

DESPITE THE CENTURIES THAT HAD PASSED, TALA ATH COULD SEE the image over and over like a flare burning against the lids of her closed eyes. The final ship at lift-off, rocket thrusters scorching the earth beneath with a fire that seemed to rival that of the distant sun. The vessel had been ancient but determined, resurrected for a final chance at glory by the last lingering remnants of the human race on Mother Earth. But for a few thousand scattered souls who with time passed on, humanity had departed for the heavens.

"Let the fools go." Declan's long-ago scorn echoed in Tala's mind in time with the vision. *"The Daoine Maith will dance in celebration at their leave-taking."*

Tala's teeth clenched down upon the memory of her friend, cutting it off.

Talk about fools, she thought. *There are none so blind as those who will not see.* But oh, the horror in Declan's proud fae eyes when the truth came clear.

At first, the Earth had rallied, unfettered by the burden of humanity's disregard, freed from the bindings of pollution. For a time, nature came again into its own as any soul would when a poison is drawn away. Around the world, flora and fauna both crept back from the edge of extinction, reclaiming the planet. Tala and her people rejoiced. Everywhere flourished such beauty as had not been seen outside the fae lands since before the advent of humanity. But eventually, in the early days of the Earth's second century without man, the first effects were felt, gradual but persistent. At first, things just leveled out, barely enough for any to notice. But then it could not be denied that fewer young were born among Earth's creatures with each decade that passed and less of fruit and flower came from nature's bounty until even the fae in their sheltered Lands sensed the lessening of all things.

In the absence of humanity's fleeting vibrancy... their passion... the spark that set them apart from all other of Earth's children, nature seemed to divest its sense of purpose. Without the humans' life force and the mage energy sloughed off from them like skin to dust—vital to the ecological balance—those left behind faded. The animals, the plants, and even the fae, though many decades passed before any acknowledged the cause. Declan had been among the first. Though not truly dead, he and others like him drifted into a stupor state from which none woke.

It could no longer be denied: Without humanity, the Earth and all it held would be doomed.

With a frustrated huff, Tala turned away from the remnants of the ancient launch pad. Careful steps led her through the crumbling infrastructure of what she was told used to be the Kennedy Space Center. Over the remains of ivy-draped concrete blocks and steel supports rusted through until they appeared like lace, across the memory of long-gone tarmac and past where a stray shard of glass somehow clung to its twisted aluminum frame, Tala's darting gaze sought out the odd jay nesting in crumbling rafters and faded blossoms long-reverted to their wild state rooted in the rich loam of rotted timbers. Her fae heart cringed at the faint yellow cast to the grasses over which she now trod. It had taken centuries, but like a field sown season after season with the same crop, something vital was missing from the Earth and everything that grew upon it.

The planet had lost a piece of its soul, and heaven help them all if it could not be gotten back.

Tala continued on her way before the ache grew too much to bear. As she did so, a trill gave her faint warning to brace before a small, compact form collided with her calves and took her to the ground.

"Beag Scath!" she scolded but with little heat. She found it difficult not to smile as the sprite wove his head fetchingly, sending his tousle of multi-hued locks bobbing. He grinned and scampered up her limbs to perch by her shoulder.

"Now, what are ye on about?" she asked, meeting the little one's orange gaze. He fussed and didn't speak, but then he seldom did. He was an odd one, bold and brash and long-beloved, having attached himself to Tala's Clan centuries before. Originally companion to the Sidhe who'd called herself Maggie McCormick, he'd glommed on to Tala's grandmother when she first became Maggie's charge and protégé. That was during the ancient days in New York when Maggie served as both pawnbroker and one of the guardians of that city. Or so Tala had been told in many a bedtime tale.

As if in reaction to her thoughts, Beag Scath reached out with a minute hand to clutch her ear while he leaned forward and brushed a kiss across her forehead.

Suspecting the wee one had not just capriciously bowled her over, Tala closed her eyes and reached out with her thoughts. *Mamó, did ye tell the little monster to dump me on my arse, or was that his idea? *

A dry chuckle and a thread of music teased her inner ear before her grandmother responded from somewhere behind her. "Sorry, lhiannon, he got away from me."

Tala tilted her head back to spy her grandmother, Kara-Anu, looking as youthful as Tala herself, with bright amber eyes and a mane of deep red hair curling around and past her shoulders. The case holding her enchanted violin, Quicksilver, hung by its strap across her back, half-hidden by those wild tresses. The grin on her grandmother's face woke an answering one on Tala's. "Hi, Mamó."

"Hi, yourself. Now up with you, my child, we haven't time for lying about."

Her brow wrinkled in confusion; Tala clambered to her feet. She had to scramble to keep up with her grandmother, who immediately set out across the clearing back toward the remnants of the launch pad.

"The memory of this place is strong even now," Mamó said as Tala came up beside her. "It might just do."

"Do for what?"

"You've cousins among the Kalderaš Clan... it's time you met them."

Kalderaš! The gypsies. The first to venture forth from the Earth, driven to the stars by prejudice and their race's curse to wander. Tala had grown up on tales of the courtship between the steadfast Jacko and his Sidhe bride, Agnieszka, of the torment of Tony DeLocosta (possessed by an evil demigod and nearly lost in that one's banishing), and endless stories both bright and dark of their children and their children's children. She had never met even one of them, born only after the Rom had journeyed to the stars. Her heart thrilled at the thought of meeting cousins born from those cherished figures. "How?" she asked, turning eager eyes upon her grandmother.

"Come," Mamó beckoned. "It's time to build new dreams of the old." And she showed Tala her vision as only the Sidhe could. Of the wandering gypsy race, finally gaining a home, of the Earth revitalized with the return of her wayward children. Of the world and all it held growing hale and whole and healthy once more. Tala's breath left her in a rush through open lips, and her eyes went wide in awe. But without question, she followed. This would not be the first time Mamó had saved the world, though few, but the fae knew the truth of that other tale. Tala had grown up expecting wonders of Kara-Anu, the mortal girl who had become both fae and goddess.

In the center of the crumbling launch pad, crowded by the memories of long-ago dreams, Tala watched as Mamó cradled Quicksilver beneath her chin and brandished her bow. And then bow arm stroked, and fingers danced until Kara-Anu's whole body moved with the power of the song. Tala's spirit calmed until she found herself first humming, then singing, drawn into the spellcasting. Melody and harmony wove about them in a dance of color and light and music such as the world had long done without. The air crackled with the gathering magic. Tendrils and sparks lit up the space surrounding them, music wrapped them in its grip with silky smooth notes that ran like fingers over their hair, raising the strands like burning clouds about their heads. Raw energy ready to do their bidding.

Together they wove a vessel of starlight and moonbeams, of sunshine and life force, powered it with resolve and bound it all tight with their will until before them rested a glittering orb stretched oblong like a grain of fat rice. A touch to the shimmering skin sent rainbow ripples across its surface. Those ripples murmured an echo of the melody woven into the craft's making.

Tala released a quavering breath. What a glorious thing.

"Are you ready, Tala?" her grandmother asked. There was a faintness to her voice that made Tala frown, but she nodded. Mamó ran her fingers along the edge of the orb, folding away a section of the skin. She held out her hand. For a brief moment, Tala could not bring herself to take it, but this was her grandmother, the undying Kara-Anu, sister to the Mother Goddess Danu herself.

Tala allowed her grandmother to aid her into the vessel of light and life. It cradled her as she had not been since she was a child small enough to fit in her Mamó's arms. Tension melted away in the warmth of that embrace. She looked around for Beag Scath, wanting to say farewell, but the sprite was oddly absent, though Tala swore she could faintly hear his cooing. With a frown, she turned her attention back to her grandmother. From where she stood outside, Mamó caressed the orb. "This will get you where you need to be." She paused to draw a cord from around her neck. From it dangled a familiar copper pendant etched with faint runes. "And this will guide you."

The medallion... it was an ancient charm that in ages past had linked a younger Kara to the gypsies before they were kin. It had been given to Mamó by one called Granddame Rose, grandmother to the demigod-possessed Tony. As it settled over her head, Tala sensed the kernel of power still nestled in those runes just as binding as the day they'd first been etched. If tears glistened in her eyes at that gift, her jaw dropped at what came next.

"And she will keep you safe," Kara-Anu decreed with a hard edge of command backing the words as she slipped Quicksilver and her bow into its case, and the case into the space by Tala's feet.

Tala did not argue, but she did ask, "The Kalderaš, what am I to tell them?"

Kara-Anu remained silent a moment, her eyes glimmering as she leaned forward, pressing a kiss to Tala's forehead. "Tell them... It's time to come home."

Previously published in *Fantastic Futures 13*, Padwolf Publishing.

TURTLES ALL THE WAY DOWN
An Alliance Archives Adventure

It was a training exercise. Just a training exercise, Kat had to keep telling herself.

The telling wasn't a problem.

Remembering? Much harder.

Checking the connectors on her harness and pack and readjusting the lay of her gear, Cadet Katrion Alexander stepped up to the line. Below her ran the path down the mountain. At key points, pennants marked off the zones she had to transverse. It seemed clear. It seemed easy. One of the first lessons they'd learned in Basic... never trust how things *seemed*.

"Soldier, is there a problem?" The drill sergeant asked from behind her, his words snapping hard against her ears.

"Sir, no, sir!"

"Then move your candy ass down that course, now!" His voice climbed higher with each syllable uttered.

"Sir, yes, sir!" Kat screamed as she barreled off the line. She was in full kit, carrying a 70-pound load, with her rifle gripped in both hands, one on the butt and one on the barrel. Her eyes tracked from point to point, assessing possible ambush. Her objective: reach the bottom on her feet, with all her gear. Her opponents' objective: knock her flat on her back and keep her there. It was called turtling, and with good reason; in full kit, when a soldier ended up on their back, the pack lifted them high enough to stranded them like a turtle on its shell.

Not hardly, Kat thought to herself. She set her jaw and moved down the path with steady caution, eyes scanning, and rifle at the ready, not for firing, but as a stave. From her left, there was a rustle. Then a form lunged out of the brush. Kat dropped into a crouch and brought up the butt of her weapon, connecting with the balaclava-shrouded attacker. A blow to the faceless opponent's chest burst the squib in the training harness. The moment the dye was released, they dropped back, hands raised, sunlight glinting off their goggles so that even then, she had no clue of the vanquished's identity.

Kat didn't care; didn't even bother to watch. She pivoted as soon as she'd confirmed the "kill" and continued down the winding path. Passing the first markers, she moved with care as she skirted boulders and other variables in the terrain. Training kicked in, and she kept her pace steady and unrushed, always confirming the space in front of her was sound before she moved into it. Halfway to the next marker, she discovered a trip-line across the path. A visual scan determined the nature of the threat. To either side of the path were deadfalls engineered to cost her her footing. She took care stepping over it before moving on.

"Come on, soldier! We don't have all day! What, do you think this is a walk in the park?"

The sudden bellow startled Kat, sending her feet skidding in the dust as her load unbalanced. There was laughter from above.

"I think we're gonna have ourselves some snapper soup for chow tonight, gentlemen!"

With a grimace, Kat caught herself and heaved back upright, forcing the sounds of the others from her thoughts. All her focus was on the course. Another set of pennants flapped as she went by. She was starting to get winded, the downward momentum working against her. It was a struggle to remain upright when both gravity and her kit kept trying to tug her down. But she did it. Because no matter how loud the hecklers got up there, they were no match for the still, soft voice in her head. Cherished and steadying. *You gonna let them get you down, baby-girl?* Kat held on to the memory of her PawPaw's words, often spoken to her when her spirits were flagging and the temptation to give up was strong.

Not. Today.

Growling deep in her throat, Kat ducked as something came at her from the back left. She pivoted and dropped in a controlled squat, kicking out with her right leg. Her opponent caught her ankle in a hard grip. Without having to think about it, Kat brought her rifle butt down, aiming for the wrist holding her tight. Her opponent released and dropped back before she connected, feigning with their own weapon. Before she could recover, a heavy weight slammed her from the right. She had to scramble to get her knee braced as she pushed back against the impact.

"Break away, Alexander! You think this is a dance or something? For Criminy's sake! Who cleared you for the corps anyway? Move it! Move it! Move it! We ain't got all day, Cadet."

Distracted, Kat caught one in the chin by an elbow jab... or maybe it was a boot. She was having a hard time telling. Sweat blurred her vision, and the double attack had her attention split. In either case, her nostrils were filled with the sweet-copper scent of blood. She spat at the assailant on her right, hoping to foul his goggles enough to get one of them off her back temporarily. Literally.

Scrambling, she broke away, lunged forward, and found herself in the safe zone; the *thwap* of the canvas pennants sounded more like another taunt. Somehow she was three-fourths of the way through... but she wasn't relaxing yet.

Suddenly, behind her, came the thud of booted feet pounding the hard-packed trail. Many booted feet. It wasn't possible to glance back past the bulk of her kit, but Kat didn't need to.

"Aw, shit!" Taking a firm grip on her rifle, she double-timed it down the slope, dodging and praying every step she went. As the incline lessened and her pursuers were still yards back, Kat let a grin slide across her face.

She never should have.

With the next stride, her right foot came down on something in the grass, hard and smooth and curved. Her foot slipped, and Kat went back, thudding hard across her pack. Her eyes closed, and her lungs struggled to draw breath, while her left leg screamed at being bent back almost beneath her. The thud of running feet stopped close by. Inwardly, Kat groaned, then slowly opened her eyes. The drill sergeant squatted down next to her, a smirk on his face.

"Shake it off, soldier," he said as he placed something on her chest. "No one makes it down that hill without landin' on their backs at least once.

"Of course... most don't have such professional help being turtled."

Kat shook her head and looked at him in confusion, only to groan again as she looked down at her chest. For a moment, she forgot about figuring out how to get up. She lay there staring into the face of a startled box turtle with a tell-tale scuff across its thick shell.

Previously published in *The Die Is Cast,* AGM Publications.

DAWNS A NEW DAY

*"I get knocked down, but I get up again.
You're never gonna keep me down."*
— *Chumbawamba*

CHARLIE DIDN'T KNOW WHERE THEY CAME FROM. WHAT THEY WERE. All that mattered was that her momma had held them dear. There were so many memories of her raising her hands mere inches from the plastic-wrapped mounds of boxes, her expression filled with awe and fear and longing in equal measure. Beneath those, the barest flicker of hope, all but extinguished.

These were remnants from a past Charlie had never seen. Never touched. No one had touched them. That was the point. The thing that made them so precious.

Part of her longed for these things. To open and explore those boxes and all they contained, driven by an insatiable curiosity. Part of her remained indifferent, not understanding the significance of those untouched objects. How could she? Charlie had never been a part of that world, the one that existed before *it* was found.

*From the journal of
Amelia Gates,
Forensic Technologist,
Circa 1 N.A.
The artifact was discovered in a pile of cooling rock at the edge of a new fissure vent on Mount Vesuvius. Markings covered the sleek tooled-metal sides, vaguely familiar, as if we <u>should</u> know them, but unlike any identifiable form of writing ever studied since the beginning of recorded history. Smooth and ageless. A timeless work of art. Clearly manufactured but by no means anyone rec-*

ognized, of materials that defy identification. The object evoked a sense of wonder in all who saw it, followed by the overwhelming desire to discover its secrets. Some said it glowed faintly green outside of direct light. They craved to touch it. Others couldn't get away quick enough. To the media, it was pure gold... even though it wasn't.

They lived in a library. At a college where Momma had sometimes taught in the before time. Not out in the open, where anyone could see them through the plate-glass windows, but in a back room—Momma called it a break room—with no windows at all. But at night... from a young age, Charlie had roamed the stacks by moonlight devouring any book she could reach. The words on the page fascinated her nearly as much as Momma's boxes. Agriculture. Science. Modern Dance. Computer Programming. Cooking. Herblore. Mathematics. Any and all knowledge drew her interest.

She explored her little world, imagining what it was like full of people doing and working on things she'd only read about. She sat at the computers and pretended they were still full of light and life and knowledge. But never when Momma might catch her.

Sometimes for hours she would sit there and turn them on and off just to watch the screen glow to life, powered by the solar panels they'd installed on the roof.

From the journal of
Amelia Gates,
Forensic Technologist,
Circa 2.3 N.A.
They didn't bomb us into the Stone Age—whoever they are... or were—but they did set us on our collective technological asses. It took us a little while to figure out what was going on. The virus spread over time, slow but steady. Unrealized and insidious. We don't even understand how it happened. How it could happen. The damage already irreparable before we even figured out

what was going on. Like any social disease, by the time someone determined how it spread the damage was done. In less than six months one hundred years of computer development began to unravel.

You would have thought the first systems affected would be those in direct contact with the artifact, but they weren't. The world had begun to deteriorate even before the object hit the testing phase. We were doomed the moment it was found. The moment the kid who fell over it picked it up in awe to marvel at his find. No one bothered with quarantine procedures. It was a thing brought up from the earth, purified by fire. Who would have thought we needed to?

At first innocuous things—like ATMs and health trackers and home PCs—glitched, then seemed to be fine. Until they weren't. Driving any car built after 1968 carried an element of risk in proportion to the number of computer chips that went into its design and their respective functions. People fell back on the old ways. Thrift stores and consignment shops and junkyards became the new places to shop. Anywhere people could find old tech. The type anyone could repair. Things that didn't need a computer degree to operate.

The attack was multipronged, we determined that much.

Things couldn't fail all at once. That would be self-limiting. Our dependency had to persist for the contagion to spread. Anything mankind touched became a carrier until every computerized system melted away like so much broken code.

Not all of our tech failed. Just anything with roots set in Silicon Valley. Like a person with dementia, the hardware worked just fine; the software... that shredded like books torn page from page. Anything networked followed. Corporate. Government. Military. International. It didn't matter. No system was safe. Not even those beyond Earth's sphere. We didn't learn that until satellites started falling from the sky. And who knows what happened to the ISS.

Our technological base crumbled as exponentially as it had grown. No one knew how to cope, knocked back into a strictly mechanical world.

⌘

Charlie had always been told never to touch the things in Momma's prohibited stash, but they called to her. Captured her attention and would not let go. They were smooth and bright and looked cool to the touch. She resisted the call for a while, but couldn't manage forever.

Once, when Momma was away finding food, Charlie crept close and pulled one of the objects from its cocoon. It was flat, like one of the handheld chalkboards she'd learned her words on, but when she touched a depression on the side bright light came from beneath the center glass. A mere touch called up pictures that moved, colorful and cute, like it was meant for a child. She was lost in the glow and the movement, hardly noticing Momma's return.

She had looked up from the tablet to see a look of horror on her mother's face. Charlie quickly dropped her gaze and thrust the forbidden object away from her. She watched Momma through her lashes as Momma snatched it up and the shock turned to awe as she swiped a finger across the screen. Within ten minutes the pictures had stuttered and gone dark, but Charlie would never forget the awe in Momma's expression or how the ever-present flicker of hope had fanned higher.

Momma had dropped the dead tablet and scooped Charlie up in a tight hug, murmuring, "Could it be that simple?" Charlie hadn't known what she meant. Then.

She remembered growing tenser as the seconds passed, her nerves on overload until she had stiffly jerked away, avoiding her mother's fleeting look of hurt as she bobbed back and forth until the stress bled away.

"Don't worry, my special child," Momma had murmured. "I understand."

Momma has been gone a while now, the life gone out of her, just like the computers out in the library. Only there was no way to turn her on and off again. All Charlie had left of her was her journal, the pages soft and creased and worn with rereading, still echoing with Momma's voice.

Charlie used the knowledge she'd gained from it to carry on.

From the journal of
Amelia Gates,
Forensic Technologist,
Circa 4 N.A.

We tried to rebuild and that is when the truth came out. It wasn't just the computer systems that had been scrambled. The virus messed with our minds, rewrote our DNA and jumbled our thought processes until anything related to computer tech read like ancient Greek.

Going off the grid was no longer a matter of choice. The preppers had a field day being right. Everyone else clambered to catch up. Alternate energy sources kept the lights on, so to speak. Factories reworked their high-tech processes and dusted off mothballed machines from a bygone age. Craftsmen of any type were once more shown respect. It wasn't enough to save us.

As a society we became brutal. Grabbing for whatever we needed. Grabbing for what we could keep. Instead of working together to rebuild, most of us went to ground, afraid of the ensuing chaos. Some helped their fellow man... as much as they were able... but the new normal terrified us.

Individually, we are capable of being noble. But humanity as a whole is horrifying when it's afraid. We could have sustained society quite well on low-tech, as we had for most of our existence, if not for our fear. Unwittingly, we destroyed technology. Knowingly, we destroyed ourselves.

It was time to remove the plastic. Time to open the boxes. It was time to honor the legacy Momma had left her because without that legacy, there was no way to rebuild. For a fleeting moment, Charlie bobbed in agitation. The stricture against touching these things firmly ingrained. But the inner conflict could not stand against her overwhelming desire to discover the mysteries those boxes held.

First, she moved everything from the room in which she had lived for fifteen years, all but Momma's stash, the large, battered linoleum table, and a single chair. Then she cleaned the space until not even a speck of dust remained, then cleaned it again. The linoleum was well beyond shining, but it did gleam.

And then she stared at Momma's legacy. Large boxes and small, the word "Gateway" emblazoned along the sides. Fitting, even if Charlie had no idea why that word was chosen. With meticulous care, she opened each one, drew out its hidden treasure, and set the box aside, careful to group the contents with the papers for each component. Monitors. Keyboards. Towers. Mice. Laptops. Tablets. Five of each, except the tablets. All untouched until now. All uninfected. Once destined to teach the next generation. Now destined to save it.

A small foundation upon which to rebuild the world.

Challenge accepted.

Without even unwrapping the manuals, Charlie set up her empire. Wires neat and orderly, components correctly and precisely placed, power source engaged. She reached for the power button, then slowly drew her hand away. Momma's written words came back to her: *the hardware worked just fine; the software... that shredded like books torn page from page.*

Alone in this back room, touched only by her hand, these computers were fine. But no matter what she did here, it would never be enough. She had to rebuild. She had to reconnect. The infrastructure was out there, blank and void and waiting, but she never could dare touch it running on the old code. She needed to rewrite the language... she needed an anti-virus.

Pushing away from the table, she went for a walk, her mind working furiously on the problem. For days, then weeks Charlie went on many walks...

From the journal of
Amelia Gates,
Forensic Technologist,
Circa 5 N.A.
–The final entry–
Society shattered like a finely balanced glass globe knocked from its plinth. Have the past five years been our crucible? Will the shards of society be reformed better or worse than what we had been? Right now all I see is a dark time, but I have begun to expect not everyone has been affected by the virus. That those on the spectrum, like my Charlie, are wired different enough to remain unaffected.

Is this our light in the darkness? I look at my daughter and wonder...

Charlie sat back hard on her heels and tracing the webbing of scars across the back of her hand to restore order to her own mind. Agitated, she resisted the urge to flutter that hand just as much as she resisted the urge to reach out and run her fingers through the pile of shards before her, looking for order in the chaos, her mind already fast at work on putting that meaningless puzzle together, no matter how pointless it might seem.

She watched the play of light and shadow on the dusty fragments, hinting at their former brilliance. The refraction of the images captured in the larger fragments. Her gaze narrowed and her hands twitched, her head going completely still as her mind dove into the enigma, followed by her hands, sorting bits of glass with short, sharp motions, heedless of the specks of blood left behind on them. Her hands sorted glass, but her mind sorted facts. So many facts stored away over what had to be over a decade of reading the scholarly treasure trove that filled her home. She was almost there this time. Nearly broken through...

Abruptly, she drew her hands back, her motions rigidly controlled as she rose to her feet and hurried to her hidden warren, seeking out the blank pages at the back of Amelia Gates' journal. Back to the pristine monitor and tower she'd dared not touch, unwrapped from its plastic and patiently waiting for the dawning of a new day. The dawning of a new way.

It was here. She had it. The start of a new way of thinking. A way out of the darkness. A way back up to the stars. And Momma so help her, when she got there, she was going to make the race responsible pay.

Previously published in *Footprints in the Stars,* eSpec Books.

A LEGACY OF STARS

"I open the door of heaven."

—The Goddess Sesheta,
The Book of Coming Forth By Day

Have you ever gazed into the heart of a star?

I have. You are blind to anything else forever after, no matter if your eyes are yet capable of seeing. The memory dazzles your vision, your mind, leaves you in open-mouthed awe at the wonder of it. No commonplace sight that the universe may offer can hope to compare.

I did not intend to alter my perception so radically. I had no choice in this.

My name is Sesheta.

It was not always, but any other name I may have laid claim to is long lost to me. Some may know... might even tell you if you ask, but otherwise, it would not occur to them, blinded as they are, by the lingering light of that star.

In darkness... I shine.

This likewise was not always so.

On the day of my rebirth, I was led to a chamber in the ship no other was allowed to access. Etched into the hatch was a single word: Library. I wondered at that as the simple portal opened. Inside was dark, near complete, but for a pinpoint of light on the far wall. The atmosphere was stale, heavy with the scent of dust, despite the steady rumble of cycled air.

"Go," my keeper ordered. A gentle shove to my back sent me forward, fearing to stumble, fearing what might obstruct my path, unknown, unyielding... but there was nothing.

"Go, child. You must. There is no other... "

He was ancient, and all to him were 'child,' no matter that I was no untried youth.

I went forward, though I could not bring myself to anything but timid steps. My breath trembled in my chest. I remember this. I can yet feel the slick skin of sweat coating me, clinging my clothes to my body, chilling any bare skin. Nothing came up hard against my shins… nothing sent me tumbling to the deck. The point of light grew closer, if no bigger.

Don't ask me how I knew. Such details simply are since I took up my mantle.

"You must look through," the keeper murmured at my back, distant in both space and my awareness. "Place your eye to the hole."

His voice sounded sad to me, but beneath that hope and dread and uncertainty colored his words. It was an echo of my own heart.

Fearful, but obedient, I advanced until my breasts flattened against riveted steel. The placement of the glass-covered hole forced my head to bow in compliance.

It was the last time I would assume such a position.

I saw everything and nothing. Every color of light flooded my vision, and all the knowledge of the universe was at my command, wrote itself into my very being until such a simple thing as a name scarce had room for itself, it was buried so deep. For an instant and forever, I heard the music to which all light dances, the singing of stars and the beating of their hearts, felt my sweat-dampened hair ruffled by the solar winds, tasted the bitter cold of space, scented by the aeons.

I saw forever in the heart of that star.

Do you wonder that I was so changed?

Tst! Pay attention!

I rose that day from where I'd crumpled with my clothes, myself, my fears burned away. I turned back to face my keeper. By the glow of my bare skin, I became aware of the pictures on the chamber walls, etched glyphs, symbols of another age at once both strange and known to me. They were obsolete, lost in the shadow of all knowledge crowding my thoughts.

I retraced my earlier footsteps, no longer timid, no longer blind, though I still could not say if the sight were that of my eyes. I stopped at the threshold where my former keeper had abased himself. I brushed my fingertips across the crown of his bowed head. The fine strands of his aged hair shimmered a moment, and the ancient gasped, his body taut and trembling.

Such is common for those star-touched.

Hair thickened, gleamed with an ebon hue recalled from long-ago years, skin smoothed, and twisted joints straightened until ageless youth rest beneath my hand.

"Rise," I told he who had for so long remain faithful, "and attend me."

We walked across the heavens, opened the doors of transcendence, ushered a great many souls. I can tell by your eyes you would ask me why, if only you dared. I will tell you. Humanity was easily lost among the heavens, without someone to guide the way.

Ages passed unnoticed. Time means little when starsong echoes in your ear.

He is gone now; in case you wonder. They are all gone, but for my remembering.

I am tired, child... and there is no other... place your eye to the hole.

Previously published in *A Legacy of Stars* and *Transcendence*, Dark Quest Books.

ABOUT THE AUTHOR

Award-winning author, editor, and publisher Danielle Ackley-McPhail has worked both sides of the publishing industry for longer than she cares to admit. In 2014 she joined forces with Mike McPhail and Greg Schauer to form eSpec Books.

Her published works include eight novels, *Yesterday's Dreams, Tomorrow's Memories, Today's Promise, The Halfling's Court, The Redcaps' Queen, Daire's Devils, The Play of Light*, and *Baba Ali and the Clockwork Djinn*, written with Day Al-Mohamed. She is also the author of the solo collections *Eternal Wanderings, A Legacy of Stars, Consigned to the Sea, Flash in the Can, Transcendence, The Kindly Ones, Dawns a New Day, The Fox's Fire, Between Darkness and Light, Echoes of the Divine*, two cookbooks: *The Ginger KICK! Cookbook* and *Auntie D's Recipes*, and the non-fiction writers' guides *The Literary Handyman, More Tips from the Handyman*, and *LH: Build-A-Book Workshop*.

She is the senior editor of the *Bad-Ass Faeries* anthology series, *No Longer Dreams, Heroes of the Realm, Clockwork Chaos, Gaslight & Grimm, Grimm Machinations, A Cast of Crows, A Cry of Hounds, Other Aether, The Chaos Clock, Grease Monkeys, Side of Good/Side of Evil, After Punk*, and *Footprints in the Stars*. Her short stories are included in numerous other anthologies and collections. She is a full member of the Science Fiction and Fantasy Writers Association.

In addition to her literary acclaim, she crafts and sells original costume horns under the moniker The Hornie Lady Custom Costume Horns, and homemade flavor-infused candied ginger under the brand of Ginger KICK! at literary conventions.

Danielle lives in New Jersey with husband and fellow writer, Mike McPhail and four extremely spoiled cats.